ABOUT THIS BOOK

One little stolen shirt and my uncle sends me to live with my dad in some weird little town in Colorado.

Ava Tate has never had what anyone would call a fairytale life. A dead mother, an absent father, and an uncle who doesn't want her. One more year of high school and she'll be able to live on her own. But after another run-in with the cops, her uncle sends her away to live with a father she's never even met before in a town she's never heard of.

How will she survive an entire year stuck in the mountains?

Ava isn't counting on meeting Toby, though. Suddenly, all the rules seem to be changing, and if she doesn't keep up, her very existence will be wiped away. After Toby tells her what she really is, Ava finds out that some don't believe her kind should exist at all. Ava must come to terms with a truth that was buried with her mother, or this paper bird will be destroyed.

HAVENWOOD FALLS HIGH BOOKS

Stay up to date at www.HavenwoodFalls.com

BOOKS BY AMY RICHIE

Willow

Fern

Ivy

Timeless

Always

Infinite

Everlasting

Lost In Flight

Found in Time

Crashing Waves

Black Dolphin

Castles in the Sand

Unspoken

Soft Spoken

Outspoken

Deceitful Whispers

Revengeful Chatter

Unforgiving Scream

Riley

Lost and Found

The Seventh Sacrifice

The Last Tomorrow

Worlds Apart

PAPER BIRD

A HAVENWOOD FALLS HIGH NOVELLA

AMY RICHIE

To my kids, you're stronger than you think.

PROLOGUE

EIGHTEEN YEARS AGO

The air was crisp with an October chill. Up ahead, he could make out the bar where Elias had asked to meet him. He still wasn't sure what this meeting was all about, but when his old friend had called, Ralph couldn't resist his desire to meet him again after so many years apart.

Elias had fallen off the grid completely, almost like he was gone from Earth, but Ralph knew better than that. Elias was one of the few angels left here that he could trust.

Inside the bar, an old country song blared from the jukebox. In one corner, a couple was so twisted up in each other, it was hard to tell where one stopped and the other began. His heart clenched a little for his Beth. If she were here, they would be in a similar position.

He quickly shook his head to dispel such thoughts. He was here to meet Elias, and then he would go home and . . . He grinned as his thoughts ran away from him again.

"Ralph," a familiar voice boomed out. A dark-haired man waved from a stool at the bar; Ralph hurried to join him.

"Elias." He smiled wide. "It's been a long time, my friend."

"Indeed it has." Elias beamed back at him. "Sit. I'll buy you a drink."

Ralph sipped on his drink while he listened to Elias talk about the town he had come from.

"Sounds pretty . . . ideal," he commented when Elias took a breath. Being an angel himself, Ralph knew what a town that offered that kind of protection must mean to Elias.

"It is," he agreed, "but that isn't why I asked you to meet me."

"Then?"

"I've been hearing some . . . rumors about you."

Ralph stiffened slightly. "What kind of rumors?"

"Word is that you've become attached to a human."

His eyes narrowed as he took a forced drink. "I don't see how that is any of your concern."

Elias's hand tightened around his drink. "I'm only looking out for you, friend. There are some who won't take kindly to your . . . transgressions."

"What exactly are you trying to say?"

"I'm telling you to end this before it's too late."

Ralph stood up from his stool. "Are you threatening me?"

"Not at all," he said calmly. "Just trying to help."

"Did Daniel send you to talk to me?" He ran a hand over his face. He was a fool to think he could trust Elias. "What I do isn't any of your business, and you can tell Daniel that too."

"I'm not here for him."

"Whatever."

"If you run into trouble, come to this town of safe haven. They might be able to help you there."

"I don't need anyone's help."

Ralph was fuming as he slid off his stool and stormed out of the bar. So Elias was doing favors for Daniel now? Who did they think they were to tell him what to do? He didn't take orders from anyone. His feet slapped against the pavement as he made his way toward the only person who offered him any comfort these days.

Her.

CHAPTER 1

I sucked in a deep breath and held it in my aching chest. Pushing my senses out, I could just make out the argument going on in front of me—on the big porch attached to an equally large farm house.

"Did you get my letter?" Uncle Ted asked the man who hadn't stopped scowling since we pulled up.

"Mail's slow here," he grunted in reply.

"If I had your phone number . . ."

"No phone."

"Ava is in the car." He jerked his thumb back to me.

From my distance I couldn't be sure, but I thought I saw the man's eyes bug out. "Why?"

"If you would have read my letter . . ." He scowled, letting his words trail off in a grumble.

"Why is she here?"

"There's been more trouble."

"What kind of trouble?"

"The girl can't stay out of jail."

I sank lower into the seat. There was no reason for me to hear this part, no matter how exceptional my hearing was. Uncle Ted and his lovely wife Jane didn't want someone like me around their perfect children. I was a bad influence.

Or so I had been told.

"Hey." Uncle Ted was suddenly back at the car, yanking open my door. "You can come out now."

"I thought you said we were coming to see my dad."

"What?" Distracted, he pressed on the trunk button that was hidden in the glove compartment. "We are," he grunted, still close to my face. "That's him up there."

I peered through the glass at the man glowering at us. He couldn't have been more than a few years older than me. Why was Uncle Ted lying?

"Come on out now," he ordered curtly, moving around to the back of the car to take out my suitcases.

Reluctantly, I pushed the door open farther and stepped out onto the unfamiliar grass. So this was where they were banishing me to? For one stolen shirt?

I really hated being a bad influence.

Uncle Ted had already dug all my things from the trunk and had most of it tucked in his arms and in his hands by the time I reached him—clearly he was in a hurry and I wasn't moving fast enough.

"I got these," he panted when I offered to help. I had little choice but to follow him back up to the house.

"Ralph." Uncle Ted reached out to the man who was obviously not old enough to be my father. "This is Ava."

Ralph's mouth fell open and stayed that way.

Now that I was closer, it was clear that something was different about Ralph, something I couldn't put my finger on. Even if Uncle Ted and Jane wanted to get rid of me, it wasn't right to just dump me off with a stranger in a town I had never heard of. We had a hard time finding the place; that should have been a sign.

"Who are you really?" I asked Ralph.

"He's your father," Uncle Ted sputtered. "I know this is—"

"He's not my dad," I cut him off. "He's too young."

"Well . . ." Uncle Ted rubbed his hand across his top lip.

"How did you find me?" Ralph asked, suddenly finding his voice again. "You shouldn't be here."

"We did get lost," Uncle Ted admitted, still not acting like himself. It must have been the stress of abandoning me when he promised his sister that he would take care of her only daughter. "There was a man—Brad, I think he said his name was—he pointed us in the right direction."

"We followed a bus," I piped in, taking pity on Uncle Ted and his stutters. I had never seen him so flustered.

Ralph's eyes strayed to me, as if he'd just remembered I was standing there. "Brad." He snorted. "Figures."

"So"—Uncle Ted cleared his throat—"anyways . . ."

"She can't stay here," Ralph suddenly snapped. "I don't want her."

Uncle Ted had the decency to shoot me a look of pity. "She . . . needs somewhere to go."

"She can go back with you."

"We don't . . ." He cleared his throat again. "She can't stay with us."

I was glad he hadn't said out loud that he didn't want me either. I mean, it was pretty obvious, but at least he didn't say it out loud.

"I'm . . ." Uncle Ted took a deep breath. "I'm sorry how this all worked out. If your mom . . ."

Was he really going to say he wouldn't dump me off here if she didn't die? If I hadn't killed her?

"Whatever." I shrugged. "Hope you and Jane . . . you know . . . do your thing." Despite how it was ending, I had lived with Uncle Ted for the last seventeen years. If nothing else, he was comfortable, and until he married Jane, he was even kind of nice.

"Yeah."

There were no tears or hugs or heartfelt goodbyes. He gave one last shrug, then slouched off the porch and practically ran back to his waiting car. If he got his way, I would never see Uncle Ted again. Feeling sad would have been appropriate, I realized. Too bad I couldn't bring myself to it.

"Hey," Ralph screamed, running off the porch after him. "I said you can't leave her here."

Uncle Ted was already pulling out of the driveway, though—without me. He didn't turn around.

"Ted!" Ralph stood alone in his front yard, screaming after the retreating car. All that was missing were the chickens and the beer-stained T-shirt, and this would be an episode on a reality TV show. "Come back here!"

Could today get any worse?

"He left," Ralph panted, stopping in front of me. "He just left."

"I noticed."

"You can't stay here."

My eyes slid closed and then opened again slowly. "I'll be eighteen soon."

"In seven months," he thundered.

It came as a bit of a shock that he knew my birthday. "Did you even know my dad?"

"Umm." He pinched the bridge of his nose. "I guess so."

"And my mom?"

5

At this, his hands dropped back down to his sides. "What did you do to get kicked out?"

"Stole a shirt." I shrugged, glancing down at the offending top. It wasn't even worth all the trouble I had gotten into, ten bucks at the most. Why didn't I just pay for it? "Is there a room in there I can use?"

His lips pursed tightly, but when he spoke again, his voice was soft. "Just until we get this figured out. A night . . . maybe two."

CHAPTER 2

I glanced around the handkerchief-sized room with mounting concern. I could just make out the bed under piles of boxes and what looked like car parts. Boxes were also stacked along the walls and blocked the closet.

This was the room he was giving me? The house was huge. There had to be an empty bedroom in here somewhere. I wasn't even going to be able to sit down, let alone use the bed and closet.

"You can, uh . . . ." Ralph ran one hand through his already messy hair. "Clear this out if you want."

"I thought you said I can't stay," I mumbled without looking back at him.

"You're here right now," he gruffly pointed out.

"True." I crossed my arms over my chest. "Where can I put all this stuff?"

"Anywhere really. There's a few rooms upstairs with boxes in them, shed out back. Where ever you want."

"Ok."

"This is the only bedroom downstairs," he explained in halting tones, "and there's no bathroom on the second floor."

"I don't need an explanation." It was still too weird to turn around and actually look at him.

"Don't worry . . . Ava," he stumbled over my name. "I'll talk to Ted. He's a decent guy—for a human."

"A human, huh?" I didn't smile at his weak attempt at humor.

"He'll take you back."

Even if Ralph could convince Uncle Ted to take me back, I didn't want to go. He had already thrown me to the curb like a bag of trash. Why would I

7

go back? Ralph knew my dad and although he didn't want me, if it was a choice between here and back with Uncle Ted's family . . .

"I'm staying here," I informed him flatly, turning just enough so I could see him in my peripheral vision.

His face paled further. "Why would you want to stay here?"

"Just until I'm eighteen."

"That's . . ."

"It's better than some of the places I've stayed." I raised my chin defiantly.

"But you were with your uncle since you were born."

Again with him knowing things about my life.

"Not always." I wasn't going to relive those memories with him, though. I just needed a room for a few months. I could figure things out and get a place of my own after I turned eighteen. I didn't have to burden anyone then.

"Why do you want to stay here?" he asked again.

"You're not much older than me. It'll be like having a roommate." That was a good enough reason.

"I'm older than I look." He raised his chin slightly. "They have good water here in town."

So far I hadn't seen much of the town. An old black man, the back of a bus, mountains that rose up from the ground all around us, and then the farm. No fountain of youth so far. "How old are you?"

"Older than you."

"Okay." I let my eyes widen in his direction. "How did you know my dad?"

"He's . . . my brother."

Another uncle.

"Do you know where he is?" Not that I was going to live with him, even if I did know where he was or what he looked like or anything about him really. I didn't even know his name. I always assumed Uncle Ted didn't know him either, but evidently he had some contact with his family.

"I need to run into town," he announced suddenly. "You stay here."

I had already planned on it.

"You can just"—he waved his hands at the room—"clear this out and . . . wait."

"Good idea." I scowled.

"Or don't." He moved his shoulders nervously. "I don't know how long I'll be." With that, he turned and darted away from me. He was so weird.

Sighing deep enough to move my shoulders, I slipped my jacket off and hung it on the door knob. Pulling a hair tie from my wrist, I quickly twisted all my honey-colored hair up into a messy bun.

Cleaning the room would be hard work, but maybe that was exactly what

8

I needed. A distraction from all the things going on around me. That's how things usually happened—I never felt like I had control over anything.

Except for . . .

I shook my head quickly. The room wasn't going to clean itself.

~

Rolling my shoulders back and forth to get the stiffness out, I sank onto the soft bed. It had been a long afternoon and Ralph was still gone. Even if he found Uncle Ted and made him come back to get me, Uncle Ted couldn't take me home—Jane would never allow it.

The more I uncovered, the more surprises the room gave me. It turned out I now had a desk, dresser, and a nice mirror. As a bonus, the closet was empty except for a few boxes on the top shelf. And it was a big closet, partially making up for the tiny room.

This would do for now.

"Hey."

I looked up; Ralph was standing in the doorway, his face suspiciously calm.

"You're back?" I asked stupidly. He lived here. Of course he would eventually come back.

"I decided that you could stay."

He must have talked to Uncle Ted. I cringed away from the thoughts of what had been said to make him look like that and change his mind so completely. I didn't want to know. "I was going to anyways."

"Room looks good."

"Thanks."

"Where did you put everything?"

"I took most of it upstairs to that first room. It was already pretty full but . . ." I let my words fall away. He had said I could put the stuff anywhere; there was no need to ramble on.

"I . . . talked to . . . the Court."

"Who?"

"You don't have to register for now," he forged ahead despite my confusion. "I told them you weren't staying and you haven't come into your . . . you know . . ."

"No." My face twisted. "I don't actually know what you're talking about."

"Doesn't matter." He scowled back. "You're fine for now."

Fine for now? Court? Register? And come into my what? Was I supposed to understand any of that? "I . . . don't know . . ."

"Just forget it." He turned away from me.

9

"Do you have any food?"

"What?" He spun back, surprised by my sudden change of direction.

"This room was a lot of work. I'm hungry."

His eyes widened briefly, then narrowed back out. "Maybe." He shrugged. "I don't shop a lot."

"Homeless people can't really be too picky," I said softly, moving past him to get to the kitchen. No matter which way I tried to look at things, I was pretty much homeless now, clinging onto the only straw I had left.

I almost felt bad for Ralph, but I was determined not to be a burden on him. Starting with making my own food.

There wasn't much to choose from. He obviously didn't cook much. I found some bread that didn't have mold on it and some lunch meat that still smelled okay; a sandwich was within my wheelhouse of culinary skills. My stomach rumbled at the thought, reminding me that I hadn't eaten much of anything since the night before. A sandwich was perfect.

Ralph watched me while I worked. I tried not to be uncomfortable; this was his house after all. He had only given me one room—a room that I had to work for—so I didn't feel guilty about taking ownership of it.

"I'm staying here for senior year," I declared, not looking at him. "Then I'll leave."

Ralph nodded. "You won't have to stay that long."

"I'm still going to." I searched the empty fridge and found a lone bottle of ketchup in the door. Good enough, I inwardly shrugged. It appeared that good enough was going to become my mantra for a while.

Not forever.

"*You won't always be underage,*" Caleb sighed, twisting one of my stray hairs around his finger. "*Soon enough, he won't be able to tell you what to do anymore. You can come stay with me.*" He smiled softly, showing off all his perfect teeth.

"*It feels like forever, though.*" I pouted, sinking into his velvety voice.

"*Not forever.*"

"Don't worry." Ralph sighed loudly, effectively bringing me back to the present and his understocked kitchen. "I'll talk to your uncle."

"You are my uncle," I reminded him.

His teeth worked his bottom lip.

"He'll take you back," he went on relentlessly. His eyes went in and out of focus as he worked out how exactly he was going to get rid of me.

I hated to burst his bubble; nothing would work, though.

"I'm not going back there." I scowled. "I don't care if Uncle Ted agrees to it or not; I'm staying. I just did all that work." I half-heartedly gestured back to the room he had lent me. "Don't worry, I won't cause any trouble here." It was hard to stay out of trouble, but I needed to. At least until I turned eighteen, but it would be better to be able to graduate.

One step at a time.

Without waiting for him to sputter any more excuses at me, I made my way back to the small room with the comfortable bed. It wasn't exactly my room, but it had all my stuff in it, and that would have to be good enough for now.

CHAPTER 3

a bird of some sort called loudly right outside my bedroom window, making my eyes shoot open. I bolted upright in bed, my heart pounding in my chest.

"What the hell was that?" I whispered to no one.

Inching my body forward, I peeked through the slit in the curtains, searching out the monstrous creature. It wasn't even fully daylight yet. A quick scan showed that I was in no immediate danger. I rubbed sleepily at my gritty eyes and let out a small groan.

Sleep was out of the question, since I hadn't actually seen anything out there. That meant it could be anywhere—plotting its attack on me. No, it would be no use to lie back down until I knew for sure that I wouldn't be killed by Big Bird.

I slid the rest of the way off the bed and shuffled out to the kitchen. My mouth dropped open at the sight that waited there.

"Morning," Ralph awkwardly greeted. "I made you some food."

"I see that."

The circular table was full of various plates of breakfast foods and even some that weren't breakfast. Sausage, eggs, toast, pancakes, pizza, jello, a bowl of butter, what looked like an entire chicken . . .

"I couldn't remember what humans liked to eat when they first wake up." He swallowed hard.

"How did you do all this?"

"I got up early."

"It's early now," I pointed out. "Did you go to bed at all?"

"I just sleep when I'm tired." His shoulders jerked upwards. "Are you going to eat?"

I slid into an empty seat at the table. There was no point in being rude, I told my still racing heart. Besides, the food really did smell delicious—better than the sandwich I had eaten the night before.

"You look scared," he noted, as I began piling sausage and toast onto my plate.

"It's not because of the food," I blurted out, suddenly remembering the killer bird.

"Then?"

"It's nothing." I had already resolved not to bother him. As long as I stayed inside where it was safe, I would be fine. It's not like birds could open doors.

"You want to go to school?"

"Today?" I poured syrup on my sausage links, mouth already watering.

"Probably tomorrow," he clarified. "In general though, you want to go?"

"Not really." I had never been very good at school.

"I thought you said . . ."

"Yeah," I sighed. "I guess I need to finish it up after all the time I've put in already."

"You haven't even started yet." His eyebrows furrowed together in the middle of his normally smooth forehead.

"I've been going since I was six." I stabbed one of the links and took half of it in one bite.

"I'll sign you up. I'm not sure how long you'll be here, so you might as well go. I think the year just started at Havenwood Falls High. I hear it's a decent school."

It was the middle of October, but good enough.

"How will I get there?" As far as I had been able to tell, Ralph didn't live anywhere close to a school, so walking was out. If there was no school bus . . . "Will I have to fly there?"

"What?" His eyes widened. "Of course you can't fly."

"I know," I said dryly. "I was kidding."

Shaking his head, he began piling his own plate with pizza and jello. "You can drive. It's not too far. Eight minutes and thirty-six seconds if you drive the speed limit the entire time. Take into account traffic"—he shrugged lightly—"I would say no more than ten minutes anyways."

He stared at me until I snapped my mouth back closed again. "You timed it?"

"Last night." He nodded. "I thought you would need to know so you can plan accordingly."

"That's, um . . ." Weird. "I don't have a car." My face scrunched up at his obvious oversight.

"I bought one for you."

My mouth seemed to be on a hinge. Realizing it was hanging open again, I snapped it shut and watched as he chewed calmly. "Are you serious?"

"About which part?"

"The part about buying me a car."

"It's just a used one." His forehead creased. "It's not a big deal. I got it from Josh over at the garage."

It was a very big deal.

"Do you have a license? I probably should have asked first."

"Yeah."

"Good." He nodded. "That's all settled then."

"Yeah." I took another bite, chewing slowly.

I did have my license—that was true enough. The rectangular plastic card was tucked away in an ugly wallet I had gotten for Christmas one year. But I knew I didn't deserve that thing. In fact, I didn't actually know how to drive very well. I had only done it three or four times.

When I turned sixteen, I was determined to prove my worth to whoever was looking. Even though I didn't have anybody willing to teach me, I didn't let that stop me. At the actual test, I freaked out and refused to even turn the car on.

It was easy to convince the instructor that I had driven perfectly—the best he had ever seen. I didn't know why people believed the things I told them, but it came in handy sometimes.

Now I'd have to drive myself to school every morning? Oh well, I could do it. It was better than asking Ralph to drive me. Time to be a big girl.

"Fine." I took a bite of buttered toast. "I'll drive myself to school."

"If you need me to take you the first day . . ." He trailed off, not quite offering.

It didn't matter, though. "I don't need you."

"Good," he grunted in reply. "It's better to . . . you know . . . rely on yourself. Makes life easier."

"So I've been told." My mom died the day I was born, and my dad left a few minutes after she took her last breath. I was pretty good at relying on myself.

"I'll go into town again today," he announced. "I can get you enrolled and stuff."

"Should I go with?"

"No," he answered quickly.

Whatever. I didn't really want to go anywhere with him anyway. It would have been nice to get a look at the school and to know where it was, but I would just do that in the morning.

"Thanks for breakfast," I said, getting up from the table. "And . . . for the car." He didn't acknowledge my gratitude, which was fine. Grabbing up my half-eaten toast, I made my way back to my room.

Now that the sun had risen properly, I scanned the place beside my window for the bird that had woken me up. Everything was quiet, though—way too quiet to be natural.

Shuddering, I hurried over to the closet and flung the door open. I randomly pulled out a pair of jeans and a pale pink V-necked tee shirt. It had been a weird morning, and the sun was barely even up yet.

CHAPTER 4

"Okay," I whispered to my reflection. "First days aren't that bad." Having gotten myself kicked out of several schools, I had had my fair share of first days. They sucked.

Taking a breath, I scanned a critical eye over my appearance. My heart-shaped face was too puffy; my lips and cheeks looked swollen, but they weren't. That was just how I looked. I was slender enough not to be made fun of at school, but I wasn't what anyone would call skinny or athletic. Curvy—that's what Caleb said. My honey-colored hair hung most of the way down my back, cascading in gentle waves. It was my favorite part of myself, even if it did sometimes border on frizzy instead of wavy.

"Good enough." I sighed deeply.

Ralph wasn't anywhere to be found when I came into the kitchen. My stomach was too full of nerves to eat, but I did manage to chug down a glass of orange juice from the recently restocked fridge. As much as he didn't want me here, it was good of Ralph to make an effort.

After one glance at the big clock above the door, I knew I needed to hurry if I didn't want to be late on my very first day. Considering it wasn't everyone else's first day, everyone was bound to notice me.

Despite his warnings, the car that Ralph had bought for me wasn't bad. A cute silver thing with no rust or dents. Four wheels, a windshield, and four doors. Seemed perfect to me.

I gripped the steering wheel tight enough to make my knuckles turn white. Driving was definitely not my favorite thing to do, but I needed to rely on myself more. I wasn't willing to burden Ralph when I could do this myself.

How hard could it be?

~

Having lived in the nearby town of Montrose, I was used to the sight of the mountains that blotted out the skyline and seemed to bring in the crisp air of fall earlier than other places, but Havenwood Falls was different. The mountains were on all sides of me as I drove, boxing me in. I expected to feel suffocated by the sight of them but was pleasantly surprised by the comfort they gave me.

The three-story building of the school came into view not long after I got into town. Relieved, I pulled into a parking spot and killed the engine. Was this my life now?

Still jittery from the drive, I made my way up to the large front doors, then to the office, where they would have my schedule and books ready for me.

Puffing out my cheeks, I pushed open the heavy glass door that led to the school office. A woman looked up when I entered, smiling pleasantly.

"You must be Ava Tate?"

"Yeah." I bit lightly on my bottom lip, willing myself not to say anything she might consider rude. Although I usually didn't mean to be, people always thought I was being disrespectful. That's the word Uncle Ted used.

Get through senior year; that's what I needed to focus on. If I got good enough grades here, I'd be able to get into Harper, a trade school back home. I knew better than to hope college was possible, but Harper offered all sorts of career choices. I could do hair, or tend flowers, or . . .

"Here's your schedule," the woman called out, bringing me out of my silent musings. "And your books." She patted a stack of textbooks, still smiling kindly.

"Umm . . . thanks," I told her, smoothing my top lip out before it got out of hand.

"Welcome to Havenwood Falls High, Ava. I'm sure you'll enjoy your time here."

Eager to get away from the talking brochure, I left the office, all my books in tow and my schedule clutched tightly in one fist.

It wasn't hard to find the row of lockers. Following the numbers, I was able to find mine and deposit my books inside. Heart hammering, I checked the schedule to see which class I had first. History with Ms. Bast. How in the hell was I supposed to find it?

"Hey there," a gorgeous girl called out, a few lockers away. Her blond hair was swept dramatically off her face. "New here?"

"That obvious?" I chuckled nervously, then immediately wished I could suck the sound back in.

"I'm Miranda Saunders." She grinned.

"Ava Tate," I replied back in the socially acceptable manner.

"You need help finding your class?"

Nodding eagerly, I held the paper out to her. "History."

"Follow me." She spun on one heel away from me. "I think you'll like this school," she called over her shoulder.

"Thanks," I mumbled, keeping my eyes on the back of her shoes.

As soon as I entered Ms. Bast's class, I knew I wasn't going to like this school. At least twenty pairs of eyes swung around to take in my loose-fitting jeans and frizzy hair.

"Ava Tate?" Ms. Bast's eyebrows disappeared into her hairline. She was gorgeous, by far the prettiest teacher I had ever had. Her tight green skirt was short enough to show off her long copper legs. "Do you have family in Havenwood Falls?"

Why was that any of her business?

"An uncle," I grunted, swallowing past the dryness in my throat.

"Also a Tate?" she continued to probe.

"I didn't ask him."

There were a few scattered giggles from the room. Ms. Bast's eyes narrowed. "You may take an empty seat at the back."

All around the full classroom, eyes kept straying back to me. It was a small school; their curiosity was understandable. No one smiled. What did I care though? It wasn't like I needed or wanted to have a sleepover with any of them.

Ralph probably wouldn't let me even if I did.

The only other person sitting in the back row with me was a dark-haired boy. He stared at me with his deep coffee-colored eyes. He didn't turn away when I caught him staring. It was going to be a long forty-five minutes.

"Don't forget to study tonight, boys and girls," Ms. Bast called from the front of the class when the clock had finally clicked down. The dark-haired boy had looked at me more than he looked at his book. "European geography test tomorrow. The map is on page 43."

She directed the last part at me. Would I be expected to take the test too? How was I supposed to know anything about Europe? I had never been outside of the United States, and I never planned to be.

CHAPTER 5

*P*ursing my lips, I tapped my pencil against an open map I was supposed to be learning for the Europe test. I had never been good at tests, and I had a feeling this one wasn't going to be any better. I had to prove myself to Ralph, though.

The rest of the school day had passed in the same fashion it had begun—a whirlwind of awkward staring and nervous smiles. I didn't return any of the smiles.

Ralph wasn't home when I got back, so I made myself another sandwich and retired to my room, where I planned to stay until I knew Europe. Even if I didn't understand why it was so important for me to learn it. I wasn't going to be going on any trips to Paris or anything. I didn't like to fly.

By the time Ralph came home, my resolve was starting to waver.

"Oh my god," I half growled at the offending maps. "I can't look at this anymore."

Outside, the sun was starting to set, creating streaks of purple and orange in the vast sky. A sudden longing to see the mountains washed over me. I could use some air, I decided on a whim. I had all night to study.

"Where are you going?" Ralph asked, when I passed the table to get to the front door.

"Outside." Wasn't that obvious?

"I'm making food for you."

"I had a sandwich earlier." We didn't need to be making habits here. I was only staying the year.

As soon as I stepped out on the porch, the hair on my arms stood up and goose bumps broke out all over my skin. The air was starting to chill, and small patches of snow were piled everywhere. I was used to the cold, though.

Something else was causing it. There was no one out there with me, and yet . . .

I squinted, scanning the semidarkness around the house. Dark, impregnable shadows lined the forest in the distance. It was probably fine, I told myself weakly.

"Why did you come out here, anyway?" Ralph asked, joining me on the porch. "I thought you were studying."

"I'm done," I lied easily.

Although obviously not convinced, he let it drop. His gaze followed my own line of sight. "What are you looking for?"

"I'm not sure," I breathed. "It felt like someone was watching me."

"Really?" He sniffed the air deeply. "Are you sure?"

"No." I straightened up, suddenly realizing how paranoid I sounded. "It was probably just the wind. Or that killer bird from yesterday morning."

"I already told you that was a rooster." He scowled, not taking his eyes from the tree line.

"I'm going back to Europe," I told him with a roll of my eyes.

"Europe?" He twisted wildly to look back at me. "Is that what he told you?"

He? "You mean Ms. Bast?"

"What did he tell you?" he sneered. "Was it some cheesy pickup line? And did you fall for him?"

"You're a really weird guy."

"What?" He blinked several times.

"Ms. Bast didn't tell me that," I informed him, my nose scrunched. "I figured it out by myself."

"I don't . . . understand what you're saying."

Was this my real life?

"I'll see you later," I scoffed, stomping back inside the house.

CHAPTER 6

I chewed relentlessly at the skin on my bottom lip. I really hated taking tests; it hardly seemed fair to make me take one on my second day. How was I supposed to learn all those places overnight? I didn't even know how to pronounce half of them.

And if I failed . . .

My chest clenched at the thought, my hand falling back down to my side. There was only one thing I could do, I decided. Ms. Bast was alone at her desk—it was now or never.

No one needed to know.

"Hi." I waved stupidly at the woman sitting behind the desk. "Can I talk to you for a second?"

"Sure." She smiled kindly.

"I was just wondering if you remembered that you already had me take this test yesterday." If I just pushed a little with my mind, she would think I was telling the truth. Then I could give myself an A . . . maybe a B.

Her head jerked back slightly at my words. "Why would I do that?"

No one had ever asked that before. Why wasn't she just agreeing with me? "Because I'm new," I stammered. "So you wanted to see what I already knew."

Ms. Bast's eyes narrowed—also something I didn't expect. "Take your seat, Ava," she ordered dryly. "Class will begin soon."

What?

"Did you really think that would work, new girl?" An amused voice chuckled behind me.

"What?" I whirled around to find the boy I had noticed the day before—the one with the deep brown eyes.

"I saw you trying to get out of today's test." He jutted his chin in the direction of Ms. Bast, who had gone back to ignoring us.

"Mind your own business." I clicked my tongue against the roof of my mouth. Fully irritated with my failed attempt, I slouched back to my seat.

"I can help, if you want," the boy offered, holding his hands wide. He had followed me to my desk.

"How can you help?" It was too late now. The bell would ring in a few minutes. "You want to be study buddies?" I widened my eyes sarcastically.

"I hate studying," he snorted. "I was thinking of something more guaranteed."

"Like what?"

"Like a list of the answers." He pulled out a narrow sheet of paper that was numbered to twenty-five. I couldn't read what it said after the numbers, but I didn't need to.

"This seems a little . . ." My tongue felt swollen. How did that happen? It was normal-sized a few moments ago.

"Brilliant?" He flashed a wide grin.

"Obvious is what I was going for," I corrected with a pronounced frown, "and risky."

"Maybe." He shrugged. "But if you don't know the answers . . ." He waved the paper in front of me. "It's up to you."

Ms. Bast had gotten up from her desk.

"Fine," I hissed. "How much?"

"No money." He held my gaze briefly.

"Then?" I prompted impatiently.

"You'll owe me a favor."

"I'll owe you a favor?" I snorted. "What is this, the eighteenth century?"

"Agreed?"

"Whatever." I shrugged, snatching the answer sheet out of his hands. "But I'm not giving you my virginity or anything."

"You're a virgin?" His eyes traveled slowly down to my feet and back up again, making my face flame hot. "That's . . . unexpected."

"What the hell is that supposed to mean?"

"Tuck that into your sleeve," he ordered as the bell shrilled, ignoring my embarrassment. He turned away from me toward his own desk. Before he went far, he turned back to me. "If you ever want to do a study session without the studying, I'm here for you, Ava." His eyelid dropped into a ridiculous wink.

"You are—"

22

"Toby," he cut me off with another small wink. "Good luck on your test."

"Find your seats," Ms. Bast called above the din of conversation. Without preamble, she handed the test sheets out and sat back at her desk. Whatever she was reading must have been more interesting than maps of Europe.

A few seats over, Toby nodded encouragingly. He was probably right. I would fail if I didn't cheat. Especially since my mind thing didn't work; I wasn't sure exactly how that thing worked, so it was impossible to know if I could fix it. Maybe I was just a normal girl now.

Kind of normal.

Fingers tapping furiously against the desk in front of me, I slipped the small paper out enough to see the tiny writing. Okay, this wasn't so bad, I thought, relaxing slightly. If I just got through this one, I'd be sure to study harder next time.

"Ava Tate?"

My head snapped up at the sound of my name. My heart almost stuttered to a complete stop when I looked up to see Ms. Bast glaring down at me. Why wasn't she still at her desk?

"Yeah?" I croaked.

"I'd like to see you out in the hall," she declared angrily.

The longer I sat in the hard plastic chair, the hotter my ears became. Why wasn't the principal talking? I had been sent to see plenty of principals, having been kicked out of several schools, and they all loved to fire up their throats and yell down to me. But this one so far had just told me to sit and wait. Maybe this was like when the police took me in—he must be waiting to question me until my parents got there.

He'd be waiting a while.

The door opened behind me, making my spine stiffen—especially when I heard Ralph's familiar angry voice. He wasn't my parent. Why would they call him?

"What's going on here?" he grumbled, sinking into the chair next to me.

"Mr. Tate?" The principal sifted through the papers on his desk, his eyes narrowed. "I thought we called Ava's father . . ." His voice trailed off awkwardly.

"I'm close enough." Ralph scowled. "What did she do?"

"It's not really a big deal," I told him nervously. This was all I needed, to be in trouble before a full week even passed. Now he would see exactly why Uncle Ted didn't want me. Where would I go if he decided he didn't want me either?

"We take cheating very seriously," Mr. Friske boomed out from behind his desk.

"Mr. Friske." Ralph smiled silkily. I had never seen him so charming. "Ava is new here."

Mr. Friske made a small grunting noise, but his stony expression softened.

"I realize that." He sighed. "I understand that she just came to live with you recently?"

"Very recently," he cooed.

My mouth fell open. Who was this guy?

"We've taken that into consideration and decided to suspend Ava, rather than expel her."

"For how long?" Ralph asked before I could find my voice.

"Two weeks."

"Suspended?" I sputtered.

"For two weeks," Mr. Friske repeated, holding up two steady fingers.

"For cheating on one stupid test?" Ridiculous. I shouldn't have even been taking a test on my second day; this was all Ms. Bast's fault.

"This is your second day at our school."

"I know." It was like he could read my mind.

"I think it's important to set a precedent here." He didn't crack even the tiniest of smiles.

"Am I supposed to know what that means?"

"We'll see you in two weeks, Miss Tate. At which time you will retake that test without cheating."

"Thank you." Ralph smiled just enough so he didn't look happy but he didn't look mad either.

I had no such luck hiding how I felt. Going by the look Ralph shot me, my thoughts were displayed clearly on my face. It was so annoying, just like Mr. Friske.

"Let's go home, Ava." Ralph sprang up from his seat, pulling me along with him—all the way through the school and back out to the parking lot.

"I'm sorry you had to come down here," I murmured, trying not to look at him.

"I'm going," he declared curtly. "I assume you're okay to drive home?"

"Of course," I squeaked.

He stared at me, unblinking, for several long moments. "Why is your heart beating so fast?"

"Wh—" As usual, Ralph caught me off guard with his words. "Can you hear it?" I pressed my hand against my chest, willing my heart to slow down. "How?"

"Hmm." He shook himself out of whatever he had been thinking and whirled away from me. "I'll see you at home."

What the hell? He was so weird.

"Whatever," I grumbled, moving toward my car. It was pretty decent of him not to flip out on me over the whole cheating thing.

My shoulders slumped at the fresh memory of trouble. Uncle Ted was right about me; I couldn't stay out of trouble. I just wasn't a good person.

"You're not going to cry, are you?" Toby called out. His tall frame was leaning casually against my car.

"Shouldn't you be in class?" I scrunched my face angrily.

"They won't miss me." He shrugged, unconcerned.

This was all his fault. "Go away."

His face fell dramatically, comically.

"That's not very nice." He jutted his bottom lip out.

"I'm not a nice person." I reached for my door handle, but Toby moved himself to be more in my way.

"I thought we were going to be friends." He grinned. "Didn't you offer me your virginity and everything?"

"You got me in trouble," I accused, trying to elbow my way past his infuriating smirk.

"You're the one who got caught."

He was right, of course, but I wasn't about to admit that. It was easier to be mad at him. "I should have never listened to you."

"I was just trying to help." He chuckled. "Passing that test seemed important to you." His head tilted to one side, obviously making fun of me.

"Move."

"Ava," he purred, flashing his straight teeth. "Don't be mad at me."

"Move," I repeated. I wasn't giving in to him. Did he think I was born last night?

"You're going to break my heart." He clutched his chest.

"Find someone else to bother." I pushed at his shoulder, attempting to make him move, since he wasn't doing it himself.

"Ava."

"I've known plenty of guys like you," I growled. "I'm just trying to get through my senior year, so stay away from me."

"That's where you're wrong."

"About?"

"You've *never* known a guy like me."

The wind changed suddenly, bringing something different to his expression. Something sinister. It happened so fast, I wasn't sure what I saw exactly.

The hair on my arms stood straight up, a ringing started in my ears, and my chest clenched. My body was telling me, very clearly, that I was in danger.

Without knowing why, I found myself calculating how long it would take me to run back inside the school. Would Toby be faster?

"Ava?"

Blinking rapidly, I shook off the strange feeling. Dangerous, really? Geesh, what was wrong with me? "I have to go home," I said thickly. "Don't follow me."

"Follow you home?" He chuckled, his eyes shining. "Why would I follow you home?"

I slid into the front seat of my car and pulled the door closed. "I'm not sure why I said that," I told him through the open window. "I'm just . . . upset about getting suspended."

"So . . . you do want me to follow you?"

"No!"

"Mixed signals"—he held his hands up between us—"that's all I'm saying."

I pushed my lips out in an exaggerated pout. It was still hard to believe that I got two whole weeks for one little test. Hopefully the school wasn't always going to be this strict. "See you in two weeks."

Moving suddenly, Toby leaned far into my window.

"I seriously doubt that," he growled. Then he was gone, leaving me gasping for air.

"What the hell?"

CHAPTER 7

*G*roaning loudly, I let my head fall backward until it hit the soft cushion of the desk chair. Ralph had dug out the comfortable chair for my studying pleasure, or so he said.

It was more for torture though. Studying was by far the worst pastime. I would rather have gone outside and dug for worms than study that map of Europe.

"Ugh." I pinched the bridge of my nose in an attempt to chase away the headache that was trying to eat my brain.

I grabbed my useless phone from the corner of the desk and glanced at the time. I must have been studying the maps for hours . . . like nine or ten hours at least.

"Forty-five minutes?" I sputtered. No way was the clock working. It must have stopped working when the signal went out.

Ralph had warned me that my phone wouldn't work this far out of town, and even in town it was spotty. The mountains made it that way. But I insisted on keeping it charged just in case.

Even though I didn't have any friends that would text me. Or call me, or miss me. Or even notice I was gone.

Rubbing furiously at my eyes, I forced my attention back to something that mattered.

Suddenly a welcome distraction came from the kitchen in the form of Ralph banging around. Grinning, I slammed the book shut and bounded from the room.

"Hey," I greeted him, careful not to show my happiness. "What are you doing?"

"I should ask you the same thing," he called over his shoulder. He was haphazardly piling groceries into the fridge. "You need to prepare for the retake. Mr. Friske said—"

"I know," I cut him off. "I got the same email." Apparently suspension wasn't enough of a punishment. I had to retake the test when I went back. "But I still have a while. I've been studying all morning."

"You have?" He frowned, putting several boxes on the counter.

"Well, I mean . . . most of it." I hadn't been awake for long, but he didn't need to know everything.

"Mmm." He nodded, unconcerned as always. Really, Uncle Ted should have dumped me off here a long time ago.

"You went shopping?" I sniffed hopefully. Maybe he had picked up a few of those bagels from town.

"I'm leaving town," he announced.

"What?"

"And I wanted to be sure you had food."

"What do you mean you're leaving town? Is it because I got in trouble?"

"No." His eyebrows furrowed in the middle of his forehead. "I'll only be gone a few days."

"Where are you going?"

"It's . . ." He cleared his throat lightly. "I don't pry into your life," he pointed out. "And this is something . . . something I don't want you to pry into."

Fair enough. "Are you coming back?"

"Yes."

"In a few days." He had already said he would be gone a few days. There was no reason to panic.

"You can't come with me."

"Yeah"—I shrugged—"I get it."

"I mean"—he sighed and ran a hand through his hair—"you aren't registered, so you can't leave town."

"Umm . . ."

"Just . . . stay close to home." His tongue ran over his bottom lip.

"Where else would I go?" I whispered. No reason to be scared. He's coming back.

"Here's some money." He laid a stack of bills on the counter next to the boxes. "Just in case."

In case he didn't come back?

"I don't think I'll need it. I'm not going anywhere," I reminded him.

Ralph crossed the room and pulled open the front door. Just before leaving, he turned back to me. "I'll be back in a few days."

"Promise?"
He smiled wide. "I promise."
Good enough.

CHAPTER 8

*M*y eyes wouldn't close. No matter what I told myself, it wouldn't work. It was too bad my special powers didn't work on me.

Outside my window, a tree danced wildly in the wind, creating shadows across my ceiling. It was the middle of the night—I really should have been sleeping. I had never felt this alone, though.

I lived most of my life with Uncle Ted, where there was always commotion of some sort. He and Jane had four small children; noise was inevitable. When things got hard there, I stayed with Caleb from time to time. He didn't have a house, and the streets never slept.

Blowing air out loudly through my puffed-up cheeks, I rolled to my side and forced my eyes to close.

"Ava!"

My recently closed eyes popped back open. Was that my name I heard? It was hard to hear anything over the thudding of my own heart. Why was I so jumpy? I was clear out in the middle of nowhere. Who was going to be out there? No one was around—not even the police could come here quickly if I called. It would take them a while . . .

I sat up in my bed. Pushing my senses out, I listened as hard as I could. I had exceptional hearing. No one I knew could hear like I could.

"Ava!"

"Oh," I hissed, letting my held breath back out. Someone was calling me; someone who knew my name; someone who knew I lived here. I couldn't just lie here and pretend I didn't hear them. Heart still pounding, I threw my blanket aside and hurried to the kitchen.

I opened the door just enough to let myself slip outside to the front porch. Even if it wasn't smart, I needed to know who was calling me. Maybe someone was in trouble out there. Maybe it was Ralph.

Squirming uncomfortably at the thought, I scanned the yard where the light from the house touched. I wasn't surprised that no one was there. It wouldn't be that easy. I hugged my arms over my chest.

The late night air was cold, even for fall. In my haste to get outside, I hadn't bothered to grab a jacket or hoodie. All I had on was a flimsy tank top and short shorts.

Goose bumps rose on my bare skin, but I couldn't be sure if that was from the cold or . . . something else.

"Don't let your imagination get crazy," I whispered firmly.

Deciding I needed the sweater, I turned back toward the house. But I stopped before I'd taken a step.

"Ava!"

"Who's out there?" I turned back to the voice. "What do you want?"

It was too dark to see much of anything past my own bubble of light, but I knew where the voice was coming from. I knew it before I ever came outside. So many children's stories centered on the evil things that lurked in the woods, ready to eat us. Every irrational fear I had ever had told me not to go one step off the safety of the porch. And yet . . .

There was someone out in the trees calling to me.

I opened my eyes as far as they would go, searching for any sign of a person or even light. I would settle for light. There were only shadows and even darker shadows. It was stupid enough to be out here at all. Was I really that crazy, to be considering going out farther?

No way.

"I'm going back inside," I told the disembodied voice in a shaky whisper. "I'm not going out there."

Very suddenly, from one breath to the next, everything became crystal clear to me. There was nothing out here to be afraid of. My whole body relaxed, feeling lighter than it had in such a long time. What was I thinking to be afraid?

A friend was out there—a really good friend. They didn't need my help. They just wanted . . . to play. Grinning widely, I skipped down the few steps and out onto the grass.

"I'm here," I called out, spinning in fast circles. "I'm sorry I was afraid before, but I'm ready now. Please don't hide from me."

A light flared to life from the center of the tree line. It was a light so beautiful that it almost hurt to look at it. Shocked, I ducked my head into my shoulder. "I know you," I whispered. "I remember."

There was only one thing that mattered now—I had to get to that light before it hid again. I had made it scared by yelling from the porch when it had reached out to me. But I would fix that.

No matter what.

Taking a quick breath, I starting running toward the tree line. A low-level panic had started in my stomach, urging me blindly forward. My foot caught on something jutting out from the grass, and I sprawled forward.

"Ouch," I hissed to the darkness. Bright spots of blood oozed up on both my knees. I didn't have time to be injured. He wouldn't wait for long.

Raising up to my hurt knees, I searched out the light. It was almost gone, I realized with a fresh rush of urgency. I could just make out the faint glow now. I had to hurry.

Pushing myself back up to two feet and mostly solid ground, I took off again in the direction of the light. It was a good thing Ralph wasn't there, I realized as I ran. He would never have let me go running off into the woods in the middle of the night.

Just inside the woods, I paused against the first tree I came to. Which way did I go now?

"Ava."

"I'm here." I looked around wildly, searching for the voice that had called me out into the night. He had to be here somewhere.

"Ava."

"I don't understand what you want me to do!" As I turned in a complete circle, my foot snagged on a clump of grass, and I lost my balance.

Laying there on the cold ground, I sucked in a deep breath and watched the stars burning in the sky above me. This all seemed so strangely familiar.

"You need to get up now."

Of course I did. Why was I lying on the ground anyway? It was cold. I rose up on steady legs, waiting for my next instructions.

"Do you see the tall tree to your left?"

I nodded. I had fallen right next to it.

"Climb to the top of that tree."

"I can't climb a tree."

"You can."

He was right again, obviously. As soon as I started climbing, I realized how easy it was. My feet found the right knobs and branches, like I had been climbing trees my whole life.

The higher I got, the more excited I felt. This, whatever it was, was the right thing to do. I wasn't even cold anymore.

Once I got to the highest branch I could get to, I twisted around so I could swing myself onto it. "There," I grinned triumphantly. "I made it."

It was higher than I expected. The wind blew stronger up here than it did on the ground; I had to grab tight to the tree to stop myself from falling. "What do I do now? I'm going to fall!"

"Jump."

"What?"

"Jump."

"No, I can't jump from up here." I peeked down and instantly regretted it. My stomach rolled at the sight of the ground so far beneath me. "I'm scared."

"Jump!"

I leaned forward as far as I was able to, then . . . I let go.

It was amazing. The wind ruffled my hair and pushed it away from my face so I could see everything that was going on around me. Everything . . .

In an instant, the fog that had held me captive lifted, and I realized that I had just jumped from the top of a tree. I was going to die. Everyone would just assume I had killed myself. I didn't even have enough breath in my lungs to scream.

Just when I was sure I would crash face first into the ground, the wind seemed to catch me and hold me in its embrace. Instead of falling to my death—I was flying. Or, at least, floating. To my complete shock, I landed softly back on the earth on two legs.

Then immediately crumpled to my knees.

My breath rasped in and out of my ragged lungs. Somehow, despite everything they had been through, my lungs and heart still seemed to be working.

I leaned forward until my forehead made contact with the hard ground. I felt like I was going to throw up, but I didn't think I could move, so I just sat there with my knees against my chest. Maybe they would be able to prevent me from falling apart completely.

What the hell had happened to me? Was I going crazy?

"Ava?"

I peeked up enough to see a real person walking toward me. At least I hoped he was real and I wasn't hallucinating again. I recognized him.

"Toby?" I squeaked out of trembling lips.

"Are you all right?" He dropped down beside me.

"No." I shook my head, my forehead swishing along the grass.

"Let me see," he ordered gently. "Are you hurt?"

"I don't understand what's happening," I choked, not moving.

"I just want to see if you're hurt."

"I think I'm going crazy." Saying it out loud was so much worse than thinking it.

"What happened here?" He gently poked my bloody knees.

33

When had I moved? "I . . . fell." Shuddering, I glanced back up the tall tree that loomed over both of us. "I fell out of this tree."

Toby's brow puckered. "I don't think you did."

"I jumped," I sobbed, letting my head fall back down. He caught me before I went all the way down.

"But . . . you didn't hurt your knees when you jumped."

"Who cares about my knees," I wailed, the sound coming out muffled. "I'm crazy. Like . . . for real crazy. I jumped out of a tree because someone told me to." And now I was blurting it out to him.

"I think I would question the sanity of whoever told you to jump."

At this, my head snapped up. "How can you make jokes at a time like this? Didn't you hear what I said?"

"I heard." He went back to examining my knees. "Do they hurt?"

"I . . . no, they don't."

"I'll help you get back home," he cooed. "You're not really dressed in enough clothes to be hanging out here in the woods."

Sobbing more, I flung my arms around his neck. "You don't understand," I explained thickly. "You don't understand what I'm telling you." I wasn't entirely sure I understood.

He must have thought I had a bad dream or something. Obediently, I got up from the ground and let Toby lead the way back to the empty farmhouse. He let me cling onto him until we got inside.

"Do you think you'll be okay now?" he asked, looking down at me in the chair he had set me in.

"You're not going to leave, are you?" Cold panic shot through my veins.

"I . . . was thinking about it. Yeah."

I clutched wildly for his hand. "Please stay here tonight," I begged.

His head jerked back at my odd request. We weren't exactly friends. The last time I had seen him, I had yelled at him to leave me alone. I didn't blame him for being surprised. I didn't know why he had been out by our farm tonight, but I still wanted him to stay.

"I don't think that's a good idea," he said slowly, prying his hand away from my fingers.

"Ralph is gone," I cried, refusing to let go. "I can't stay here alone. What if . . ." My eyes darted back and forth. Saying anything else about hearing voices would scare him away for sure. "What if I have another bad dream?"

"You had a dream?" His eyes narrowed as he watched me freak out.

"I . . . don't know what it was," I admitted. "It's not like any dream I've ever had before. But . . ." It must have been a dream. Why else did people hear voices in the middle of the night—voices that wanted them to die?

"You don't look so good."

Even though I knew I shouldn't cling on to an almost stranger who gave a bad vibe, I couldn't stop myself from holding on to his arm so he couldn't leave me.

"To be fair," I croaked, "I did just fall out of a tree." Or jump, I silently corrected.

"You really want me to stay?" His dark eyes searched my face. "I thought you wanted me to leave you alone."

"I don't want to be alone tonight. I don't know Ralph's number." Not that I could call him even if I did know it.

"I doubt he has a phone," he chuckled weakly.

"You know him?"

Toby pursed his lips out. "I'll stay here tonight," he declared suddenly. "If you're sure you want me to."

"I do." I nodded quickly. I didn't want to be alone, and Toby was here already. It wasn't like I knew anyone else in town.

"Okay." He tried to straighten back up, but I was holding him too tightly. "You can let me go. I promise I won't leave."

My tongue darted out to glide over my lips. "I'll make a bed up on the floor."

"Are you going to let go of me first?"

"I don't know."

"You're safe," he soothed. "I promise you're safe."

He was making an awful lot of promises to me, but what good were his words? I didn't trust him at all.

"We can go together." I jumped up from my seat. "My room is this way."

Not giving him much choice, I pulled him into my room. Only after the door was shut behind us did I let go of him. If he tried to bolt, the room was small enough that I could get to him before he got the door open. I set to work quickly making up a blanket bed on the floor next to my real bed. It was too small to share, and I wanted to sleep next to Toby.

If I heard the voice again, he wouldn't let me follow it. Probably. I really hoped so, anyway. But what did I know about Toby? Not even his last name.

I hurried to swallow my panic before I got crazy. He was better than no one; that was the one thing I was sure of.

"We can both sleep here." I scurried under the top blanket and patted the place next to me.

"Are you sure Ralph won't be back tonight?"

"He said he'll be a few days."

"Where did he go?" Toby eased himself under the blanket beside me, still fully clothed.

35

Maybe it would be better if he took some of his clothes off, I thought frantically.

"Don't you want to be more comfortable?" I asked in place of an answer. Willing my voice back to normal, I tried again. "You could at least take your shoes off."

"I'm comfortable," he grunted, rolling onto his back—not looking comfortable at all. "You try to sleep."

In a childish gesture, I linked my pinky with his and held it tight. "Just . . . you know . . . in case," I panted.

"In case of what?" I saw his eyebrow shoot upwards to join the lines on his forehead.

"In case you decide to leave."

"You think this is going to stop me if I really wanted to go?" He tugged lightly on our entwined fingers.

I knew he was right, of course. Sniffing lightly, I scooted closer to him. I still wasn't sure what had happened to me out there. It wasn't a dream, though. It was real. But if it was real . . .

"Hey." Toby moved so he was halfway on his side, looking down at me. "Are you crying?"

"No," I lied.

"Hey," he said again, nudging me with his shoulder. "You don't have to be afraid."

"I'm not," I choked.

"He wasn't going to hurt you," Toby's voice dropped to a whisper in the night.

Without meaning to, I copied his volume. "How do you know?"

"He only meant to show you the truth."

"He wanted me to die."

"Never." In a surprisingly gentle movement, he reached across our joined hands with his free one and wiped away a tear that had escaped my eyes. "Try to sleep. I won't leave."

CHAPTER 9

$\mathcal{M}$y forehead furrowed dramatically before my eyes were fully opened.

"Oh my," I groaned, rubbing away the lines on my head and by my eyes.

I had had the weirdest dream ever. A strange voice in the woods, climbing a tree, then jumping from the tree. And Toby had been there too. In fact . . .

"Morning," a deep voice greeted me huskily.

My eyes popped open. "What are you doing here?"

A grin splashed across his face. "You wouldn't let me leave." He winked. "You were all over me last night."

"I was not."

"You made us this nice little love nest." He patted the blanket we both seemed to be laying on.

"Why are we on the floor?" Scrambling backward, I untangled myself from the blanket and plopped heavily on the bed. "Did you stay the night here?"

Toby leaned back against the pillow, his smile growing with every awkward second that passed.

"Don't worry," he taunted, "you still have your virginity."

My mouth fell open. All I had on were my shorts and tank top I slept in. Definitely not something I wanted Toby to be seeing me in—let alone sleeping next to him in. What in the world had happened last night? "But why are you here?"

"I told you." He propped himself up with one hand. "You wanted me to stay."

"I mean"—I breathed deeply, hoping he couldn't see how hot my face became—"how do you even know where I live? How did you get out here?" I didn't call him. We weren't friends. Why was here?

His grin slipped. "I came out here to talk to you."

"About what?" My eyes darted to the closet. If I got up now, it would just bring more attention to the fact that I had very little on. It was probably better to wait until he left. If I didn't get up at all . . .

"It doesn't matter right now." He jumped up from the floor and moved to the door. "Get dressed. I'll make breakfast."

"No," I said quickly, holding up one hand. "You don't need to make breakfast. I'm good."

"I'm hungry." He shrugged. "I was stuck out here all night, watching you sleep."

Heat spread through my cheeks. "Watching me sleep?"

That wasn't creepy or anything.

"You're so cute when you sleep." He chuckled. "Until you started snoring." He shuddered dramatically. "I feel sorry for your future husband, having to sleep next to that every night."

My eyes popped open. "Are you serious right now?"

Forgetting my embarrassment, I sprang to my feet and hurried across the room to help him out of my room.

Toby's eyes dropped to my knees. "Do your knees still hurt?"

"Just get out," I hissed. I knew exactly what he was trying to imply, and I also knew it wasn't true. Nothing had happened . . . at least nothing like that.

"I was just asking."

"Now. I need to get dressed." Laughing loudly, he finally left so I could slam the door after him. "Holy . . ." I leaned my entire body against the cool wood of the door.

How could he be here? Last night was a dream—I couldn't even remember most of it. There was a voice calling my name, and I followed it. Like an idiot. Where did Toby come into it?

"Hurry up." He pounded on the door, startling me upright.

"I thought you left."

"Nope. I'm waiting for breakfast."

With one more sigh, I hurried across the room and grabbed the first clean clothes I could find. It only took a few minutes to change and pull my hair back into a loose ponytail. Normally I would have changed in the bathroom so I could clean up, but I needed to be dressed before I went out there, since Toby didn't appear to be leaving.

Toby chewed loudly, I noted as I watched him shoveling spoonsful of cereal into his mouth. I had never been much of a cook, and he wasn't picky, so a box of sugary cereal and a gallon of milk was good enough for breakfast.

At least for him. I didn't eat.

"Aren't you hungry?" he grunted around a full mouth. "This stuff's not bad. Ralph knows how to pick cereal."

"How do you know I didn't pick it?"

He shrugged.

Toby seemed to know entirely too much about me and Ralph, considering he was just a boy at school who had convinced me to cheat.

"I'm not hungry." I sniffed. He needed to hurry up and go. I really wanted a hot shower and some time to think.

"What do you remember from last night?"

"Hmm?" I sat up straighter. "I know nothing happened between us," I snapped. "So don't even try spreading rumors at school."

"You were in the woods when I found you," he reminded me. "Do you remember what happened to you out there?"

"I was in a tree." I swallowed hard. "At the very top."

"How did you get up there? Do you remember that part?"

I couldn't tell if he was making fun of me or not. "I climbed up."

"To the top?"

"In my dream," I hurried to clarify. "I climbed up and then I fell out."

"You didn't fall," he argued.

"I jumped." I cleared my throat. "But I wasn't trying to kill myself, so you don't need to tell Ralph or anything."

"You flew." He took another bite, as if he hadn't said something ridiculous.

"I can't . . . fly." Even if I could in my dream, Toby wouldn't have seen that part.

That's all it was. A dream. Toby found me at the end of that dream, when I was laying on the ground and confused. If I really did ask him to stay, I was grateful he did. But I didn't want this to get around. Crazy and a slut—all in one night.

I'd had worse nights, I inwardly shrugged.

"You weren't dreaming"—Toby caught my gaze and held it—"and I think you know that."

"I . . ." I swallowed again. He was right that it felt real, but then again—it couldn't be real. Maybe I was still asleep, actually. "I don't know anything right now." I really wished Ralph were home.

"Well I do know. It wasn't a dream."

My eyes narrowed. "How do you know?"

39

How in the world could he be so sure? He hadn't been inside my head. He didn't hear that voice.

"You heard a real voice."

"No, I didn't." I closed my eyes. The world seemed to be going in and out of focus, changing from the things I knew into the things that couldn't be true.

"Ava."

My eyes snapped back open.

"I was the voice, so I know it wasn't a dream." He finally put his spoon down and leaned across the table, his eyes boring into mine.

"There's no way . . ." But maybe I had already known. I saw a flash of it at the school, didn't I? "Why would you want to kill me?"

He sat back in his chair again, huffing a deep breath out through his pursed lips. "I already told you," he grumbled, "I wasn't trying to kill you."

My eyebrows lowered on my forehead. "You called me from my bed to go out to the woods and climb a tree. Then you made me jump out of the tree."

He glanced up, his expression dark. "I guess so."

"But not to kill me?" Yeah, right. If he really did do all that, why did he stay the night?

"It's getting awfully boring having to keep telling you the same thing over and over again." He tapped the table with several long fingers.

"This all . . ." I ran my tongue across my bottom lip, trying to think of a good word to describe what this was. Weird seemed too tame.

His stormy expression suddenly changed. "You can't go and tell Ralph that I tried to kill you," he hissed with a strong hint of desperation.

"He's not here." Obviously.

"When he comes back," he clarified quickly. "You can't tell him that when he comes back."

"I'm not going to tell him about any of this." He already didn't want me to stay with him and then he got called to the school because of me. I wasn't adding any crazy to the table as far as Ralph went. "He wouldn't believe me anyway."

"You're probably right." He shrugged, going back to his cereal. His eyes kept flickering to my face.

"What did happen last night, though?" I carefully avoided eye contact.

"We've already—"

"No," I cut him off. "I mean, how did you do all that? And how did I . . . not get hurt when I jumped?"

"Are you sure that you're ready to know?" He shifted his gaze back to my face, making me squirm uncomfortably.

"Of course I'm ready," I tried to say bravely through my clenched teeth.

"It's because you're a Nephilim."

Was that supposed to be some grand reveal? I had no idea what that meant. Was that someone who walked in their sleep? Now that I thought about it, I might have heard of that before. "A what?"

"You have a human mother . . ."

Obviously.

"And your father is an angel."

"How do you know my father? I don't even know my father. And he can't be that great . . . he left me with Uncle Ted." An angel? That was going a bit far and it had nothing to do with hearing voices.

"I mean," he said forcefully, widening his eyes at me, "he's an actual angel. Wings and everything."

"That's . . . stupid. There's no such thing."

"Well . . ." He shrugged. "He's fallen, so the wing thing is iffy."

"I . . . you're not making any sense."

"Your dad is an angel that fell to the earth. Your mom is human. That makes you Nephilim," he explained slowly, in choppy sentences.

Half human, half angel? I had never heard of a person like that. But maybe that explained things. People believed me when I told them things— things that were very clearly not true.

"You tried to use your compulsion with Ms. Bast," Toby echoed my thoughts. "To pass your test."

I knew what he meant without the prompting. "It didn't work."

"The school is warded against that sort of thing."

My eyes widened. "Is everyone at the school Nephilim? Are you?"

"No and no."

"But you said . . ."

"I said you couldn't use any sort of magic or powers at school."

Magic? Just what kind of school did I go to now? Did Ralph know? Ralph. "But wait." I held up my hand. "Ralph and my dad are brothers."

"That was a lie."

"Then tell me the truth," I demanded, my breath making my voice raspy.

"You already know the truth, Ava," he said softly, so softly that I barely heard the words. If I hadn't been staring at him so hard, I might have missed them. "Ralph is your father."

"He's an angel?" Because he seemed so normal. And way too young to be my dad. "Uncle Ted," I recalled out loud, "he said Ralph was my dad. But . . . how did he not know he was too young? It's not possible."

"Ralph can be whoever the other person needs him to be. It's part of our charm."

"Why does he look young like that for me?"

"Doesn't work on you."

It was all too much. "You're an angel like Ralph?" He nodded. "What do you look like, then?"

"I don't use any sort of glamour." He grinned. "I like being young."

No one could like high school that much.

"Anyway." Still grinning, Toby pushed his chair away from the table and stood up. "I have to be going."

His words shook me out of my stray thoughts and exploding questions. "You're leaving?"

He grinned wickedly down at me. "I know you're infatuated with me now, but I can't move in here." There were too many things rolling around in my head for me to be annoyed. He must have seen the panic clearly on my face, though. "I'll be back soon," he assured me with a roll of his eyes. "Take a shower, try to relax."

"Relax," I sputtered. "How am I supposed to relax?"

"Read a book or something." With one final wink, he was gone.

Left alone at the table, I sucked in a quick breath and tried to hold it in my broken lungs. It was no use.

"What just happened?" I gasped. Toby couldn't just tell me stuff like that and then leave me alone to deal with it. It wasn't right.

How could this be real? I had never heard of Nephilim. And angels? Weren't they women in white dresses that you put on the top of Christmas trees? Was I going to believe that Ralph was an angel?

But I couldn't deny that I was something. I had always known there was something different about me.

Uncle Ted knew it too.

He avoided touching me at all costs; I used to think it was because I killed his sister. She died giving birth to me. Of course I was to blame. Now I wondered if that was the reason he didn't like me. He must have known I was different, and he was afraid of me.

Afraid.

Tears gathered in the corners of my eyes, making them sting. Ralph shouldn't have left me there with him all those years ago. He should have realized that a human would never be okay with raising someone . . . like me.

I had never given my absent father much thought. He was always someone from a fairy tale—not tangible. I was more right than I could have imagined.

"Okay." I shook my head to dispel the negative thoughts. They never did me any good. "No point sitting here crying," I told myself firmly. Tears wouldn't change anything.

I needed to stay busy until Toby came back . . . or Ralph. He had a lot to answer for once I saw him again. Hopefully he didn't ghost me again.

Sniffing lightly, I rose up from the table and closed the cereal box that Toby had been eating from. It was some fruity crap that Ralph bought for me. He must not have realized I wasn't a little kid anymore. Although age didn't seem to hamper Toby any.

I stowed the box back in the cupboard and gathered the dirty bowl filled with used milk. With a nod of my head, I ran water over the dishes, happy to have something to do.

CHAPTER 10

*O*utside my bedroom window, the sky had gone from purple to dark blue to black while I sat at my desk and pretended to study maps. The curtains were pulled back so I could see if any cars happened to pull into the driveway. The aspen trees formed a nice little cocoon around the house, effectively cutting me off from the rest of the world. It was like Havenwood Falls was an entire other planet.

It had been a long afternoon, long and boring all on my own.

A knock sounded on the front door, taking the rest of my attention away from the map. I had been waiting for Toby to come back all day. He had promised he would come back.

Hopefully that was him.

As if I were a jack-in-the-box, I sprang up from my seat and hurried out to the kitchen.

"I'm coming," I yelled, just in case. *Don't leave, Toby.*

It wasn't my dark-haired prince though. It was Ralph. Rolling his eyes, he gave me a sheepish shrug.

"Can't find my house key," he explained by way of an apology.

"Dad!" My gasp came out before I could stop it, surprising us both.

Ralph's eyes narrowed before he slipped past me into the kitchen. "Dad?" he grunted.

"I just . . . I'm surprised . . . I didn't expect you to be here yet," I stuttered, embarrassed by the accidental affection.

Ralph set his bag heavily on the kitchen table and crossed over to the sink.

"I don't mind if you call me Dad," he said with his back to me.

"What?"

"You know," he turned back around, his eyes darting everywhere but at me, "if you want to call me Dad, I'm okay with that."

"Ummm . . ." *Dad* didn't feel right. I had never called anyone Dad before, and I wasn't entirely sure I could start now.

Without waiting for an answer, he turned back to the cupboards and began pulling out boxes of food. "It's not a big deal either way." Although he tried to sound nonchalant, I had to wonder if he was hurt by my hesitation.

If Toby was right, though, Ralph was an angel—a full-blown angel. How old was he? I already knew he wasn't as young as he looked. Why did he care what I called him? After my mother died and left me alone on the earth, Ralph hadn't come for me.

"Were you bored out of your mind here?" he asked suddenly, bringing my attention back to his small kitchen.

"Not really." Maybe he wouldn't notice the airiness in my reply or the way my heart pounded at the thought of the past day. "It's all right here."

"Oh yeah?" His hands paused on the loaf of bread he was reaching for. "Any return of the killer chicken?"

"Very funny." I rolled my eyes. "How did your trip go? Did you . . . get whatever you needed done?" I still had no idea where he went, and he still wasn't giving me any clues.

"Undetermined."

"Am I supposed to know what that means?"

"Do you want some food?" he offered. He was really good at avoiding my questions. It was so annoying.

"It's late."

"People still eat when it's late," he grunted. "Don't they?"

Would it be weird to ask him if he was an angel? Would he tell me the truth? What about Toby—did he know Toby?

"Some . . ." I swallowed hard over my awkwardness. "I'm sure that some people do. Not everyone is the same."

Ralph's eyes bored into mine, making my pulse speed up again. "What kind of person are you, Ava?"

"A tired one," I muttered, shifting my eyes away. "I'm going to bed."

"Okay."

"I'm glad you're home." The words tumbled over each other in an effort to get out of my mouth.

"Yeah."

I turned away and crossed to my still-open door.

"Ava."

"Yeah?"

"You want to go get a coffee with me tomorrow at Coffee Haven? It's a nice little place in town."

"Sure." I shrugged slightly. "I'd like that."

~

The line at Coffee Haven was already almost to the door by the time Ralph and I walked in. A few eyes flickered our way, but most people were more interested in their own coffee orders to give us much notice.

"It's cute in here," I whispered happily to my quiet coffee date. "Very . . . small-town vibe."

"It has good coffee," Ralph commented in his usual gruff way. "Some of it's a little frilly."

Ralph was probably a black coffee kind of man, I decided, crossing my arms over my chest. Behind the counter, a girl who must have been part Japanese was smiling wide at a guy stuttering over his order. The girl was really pretty. I didn't blame the guy for being distracted. As I watched, she twisted her finger in her long hair and laughed out loud.

"What kind of coffee do you drink?" Ralph asked awkwardly, with enough eye contact to give the illusion that he actually cared.

"I'll probably just get some hot chocolate." I had never liked the taste of coffee. I could never resist a good coffee shop though.

"I heard the blueberry scones are quite good," he offered.

"Scones?"

His eyes widened. "That's what I heard," he repeated.

"What will it be?" the girl behind the counter asked when it was our turn to order.

"Hot chocolate and a blueberry scone." What the hell, I mentally shrugged. I noticed the small name tag pinned to her shirt read *Harlow* as she spun away from us and prepared our order.

Despite his advice, Ralph skipped the scone and only got a small black coffee.

"Here's a seat." He gestured at an empty table, where we both sat. The hot chocolate was delicious and perfectly coated the back of my throat.

"You were right about this place," I whispered, leaning across the tabletop. "It's perfect."

"I'm glad you approve."

Actually, the whole town of Havenwood Falls was nice. Even if it did look like an entire pumpkin patch had thrown up in the middle of town square. "Halloween is no joke around here, huh?"

Ralph chuckled at the sight of witch decals on a window. "Comes with the territory, I guess."

I knew the people in Havenwood Falls weren't exactly normal, but I didn't really know much about them. Being trapped out there with Ralph on his stupid farm didn't exactly do any favors for my social life.

For the first time in recent memory, I missed going to school. At least there, I had an opportunity to talk to people my own age. And if I was being honest . . . I wanted to see Toby again. I hadn't been able to talk to him since he told me I has half angel.

Why didn't he come back like he promised?

Behind me, the door opened to let in a gust of chilly morning air. The hair on my arms stood straight up, but it didn't have much to do with the cold.

Already knowing who had walked in, I whirled around and saw Toby standing just inside the door. Our gazes locked for several long hours—or maybe it was just a few seconds. Either way, excitement coursed through my veins. I could hardly sit still in my chair. Every nerve inside of me stretched tight, waiting to snap. I wasn't going to be able to sit there; soon I was going to embarrass both of us and throw myself at him.

"What the hell is he doing here?" Ralph grumbled. I had practically forgotten he was there with me.

"Who?" Tearing my eyes away from Toby, I looked to see who Ralph was looking at. He was staring right at the door. "Do you know Toby?"

His gaze moved swiftly to me again. "How do you know him?"

"He goes to my school."

Ralph nodded slowly.

"And he stopped by while you were gone."

His face fell almost comically. "At our house?"

Despite his outrage, my ears burned at his pronoun choice. Our house? "Yeah. He wanted to help me . . . study." I had never been a very good liar when it really counted. "I'll just go talk to him real fast."

"No way." He slammed his hand on the table between us, making me jump.

"What do you mean, no?" It wasn't like we were going to start going at it here in Coffee Haven. In fact, we hadn't kissed yet at all.

"You're not talking to him."

"I'm just going to—"

"Hey," Toby's familiar tone said from above us. I didn't even realize he had moved away from the door, and now here he was right next to our table. "Nice to see you again, Ava."

"We're leaving," Ralph growled, popping up from the table. "Let's go," he ordered me, without taking his eyes away from Toby.

"I'm not finished with my scone."

"Take it with us."

Mouth opening and closing like a fish, I helplessly followed Ralph from the shop. Toby didn't move from his place.

CHAPTER 11

"*Y*ou're not allowed to see him," Ralph thundered, his words vibrating against the walls in our cozy little kitchen. "He should have never been here in the first place." His nostrils flared as he glared wildly around the room. "What did he do to you?"

"Nothing." I wasn't about to tell him about the whole tree-jumping thing.

"Never"—he put his finger out toward my face—"ever talk to him again."

"You can't tell me who I'm allowed to talk to."

"Yeah, I kind of can."

"Why?"

"In case you've forgotten"—he rounded the table to put himself closer to me—"I'm your father."

Oh, he wasn't actually going to pull the dad card on me, was he? "Why do you not want me to talk to Toby?"

"He's toxic."

"Uhh . . . could you be a little more specific?" I raised both eyebrows in his direction.

"I said no."

What a dick thing to say.

"You are ridiculous," I huffed. More irritated than I could handle, I turned on my heel and disappeared inside my room, slamming the door behind me.

If this was what having parents was like, I was better off without them.

"Ava," Ralph yelled, pounding on the door. "Come back out here; we weren't done talking."

We were done talking all right; maybe I would never talk to him again.

Did he think after seventeen years, he could just waltz back into my life and tell me who I was allowed to talk to? Did he think I was seven years old?

"Don't act like a child," he continued to bellow through the wood. "There are things you don't know about him."

Of course there were things I didn't know about him. We had just met and he told me I was half angel and that he and Ralph were angels—there was a lot I didn't know. But that didn't mean I didn't want to know.

"Come out so we can talk."

I took a deep breath and blew it out forcefully. Hiding in my room was immature—he was right about that. And maybe he would be able to answer some of my questions. Even if he didn't, there were a few things I had to say to him.

Flinging the door open, I stomped past him back out into the kitchen. "What do you want to talk about?" I snapped.

"You know what you are." It wasn't a question, but I still nodded. "And you know what I am."

Uncomfortable, I crossed my arms over my chest. "Toby said you're an angel."

Hopefully he wouldn't hear the fear as it gulped down my throat, or the way my heart galloped away inside of me.

"He's right," Ralph nodded.

So, he was finally going to open up and tell me the truth—but did that change anything? Not really. I still wasn't human. I was still living with my nonhuman father in a town full of people who had something to hide.

Most importantly, it didn't change the way I felt about Toby.

"Do you know why Toby was kicked out?"

"Kicked out of . . . Heaven, you mean?" My eyebrows puckered at the implications his words stirred up. "It never really came up."

"Angels aren't kicked out for just anything, you know," he huffed, his eyes wide with anger. "It has to be something serious."

"Okay." I let my arms fall back to my sides. "Should I sit down for this story?"

"This isn't a story, Ava," he growled. "This is serious."

"You've already said it was serious." I held up one hand to stop him from saying useless things. "What happened? What did he do?"

"Violent crimes against humanity." He said it like a declaration, like the information should have shocked me, but truthfully, I didn't know what that meant to an angel.

"I'm not sure what . . ."

"Toby isn't a nice man," Ralph continued to explain. "His idea of a good time is to torture humans."

"How?"

"Set their things on fire, confuse them on the roads, make them think they're crazy—fun things like that."

"He's not like that now." I shook my head back and forth.

"You have no idea what he's like now."

That day at the school, out in the parking lot, I had felt a vibe from Toby —an evil vibe. And then that night when he called me from my bed. Toby made me climb a tree to the very top and then made me jump out of it. How many times had he done something like that to other people?

Enough times to be kicked down to Earth.

"I don't care." I raised my chin. "Nothing you say is going to make me stay away from Toby."

"You're grounded."

"What?"

"That means you can't leave this house."

"I know what it means. You can't ground me."

"Yes, I can," he panted. "You're not leaving this house again without me. Not until your suspension is over."

"That's . . . insane."

"Grounded," he said again, pointing one long finger at me. "Don't even think of going out to meet Toby. Not now, not ever."

~

The trees surrounding Ralph's farmhouse were thick, making it look dark even in the middle of the day. Since it was October, it was cold in the woods —really cold.

Shivering, I pulled my thin sweater closer to my body. It didn't seem this cold when I left Ralph's house not more than ten minutes ago. He had left to make a run to town, leaving me with the most freedom I had been allowed for days.

I was out the door before his car was completely gone from the driveway.

Toby had played a starring role in my dream that morning. He told me to wait for Ralph to leave and then to come meet him. Even though he gave good directions in the dream, it was proving more difficult to fight my way through the trees than I expected.

"As soon as you clear the woods, you'll reach Devil's Peak. I'll be waiting for you there."

Apparently, Devil's Peak was a great big rock where teenagers went to make out years ago, until a flood nearly wiped it out. Now the ground was uneven and dangerous, so it wasn't seeing any more action.

51

Just when I was sure I was going to be lost in the woods forever, the foliage opened up to a flat piece of land. Not more than twenty feet away was a lone rock jutting from the ground, and on top of that stone was a familiar dark-haired boy, grinning at me so wide that his eyes crinkled.

"Toby," I breathed. "Finally."

"Well lookee there"—he whistled low through his teeth—"if it isn't my own little paper bird."

"Paper bird?" I hurried to cross the distance that separated us.

"Half bad-ass angel and half fragile human."

"Tsk—not all humans are fragile," I said, tilting my face up toward him. It was like we had known each other for years instead of mere days.

"I've missed you," he admitted, his voice dipping low.

"I've been on house arrest."

"What did you do?"

Ralph wasn't mad because of something I did; he was mad because of Toby. He was mad because of all the evil things Toby had done to get himself into trouble.

And because I insisted on defending him.

"Ralph told me about you," I blurted, trying and failing to pull my eyes away from his perfect face.

"That I'm an angel?" He wiggled both eyebrows.

"He told me"—my tongue slid nervously across my bottom lip—"why you were kicked out."

Toby's grin froze, then faltered. "Did he, now?"

"Yeah, and he told me I'm not allowed to talk to you. He said you're dangerous." Maybe not in so many words, but the implication was obvious.

"I don't . . ." He cleared his throat uncomfortably. "I haven't always liked humans."

"Oh."

"I found some needed to be . . . taught a lesson."

I tried to imagine the avenging angel that Toby painted.

"What did you do to them?" I whispered.

"Only what they deserved. Eye for an eye, you know?" I watched his teeth work against the loose skin on his lip. "Humans can be vile creatures."

I took a deep breath, then moved to wrap my arms around his waist. "Lucky for us," I said as loud as my voice would go, "I'm not human."

"I've learned a lot since those days." He wrapped his arms around my shoulders to hold me close to his body. "I don't mind most humans now."

"Most?" I squeaked.

"There are some who annoy the shit out of me." His deep laughter vibrated against the side of my face.

"Despite my father's best efforts, I like you." Keeping my face buried in his chest, I waited for my heart to settle down before looking up at him.

The look on his face didn't do my nerves any favors.

"I like you too." His voice had turned husky, somehow sexier than any other sound I had ever heard in my life.

"What if Ralph doesn't let me see you?"

"What is he going to do, tie a blindfold around your eyes?"

"Sounds kinky." I tried to raise one eyebrow, but I might have failed.

"Mmmm."

His lips turned up into a small grin just before they moved close enough to press against mine. Tiny lights exploded behind my eyes. It was like I had waited my whole life for this moment with Toby at Devil's Peak.

CHAPTER 12

I couldn't seem to let my eyes relax enough to even blink as I watched the brunette across the table from me pulling stuff from her oversized bag. Things that I didn't recognize. Things she needed to give me a tattoo. An actual tattoo.

Tempers had been heated with Ralph and me on the home front after my forbidden outing with Toby. For weeks, the two of us barely spoke at all. Going back to school had come as a blessing—both to get me away from Ralph and so I could see Toby again. I was worried for a while that Ralph and I would spend the rest of my senior year in silence, but then one day, he made breakfast.

Right at this very table, we ate bacon and let our disagreement dissolve on its own. Although we didn't talk about Toby anymore, we did talk about other things. It was strange to me, discovering how much I had in common with a father I never knew until a few months ago.

And now this.

I came home from school, and Addie was in our kitchen, waiting to give me a tattoo that she said I needed in order to stay in town.

"You ready?" She wiggled her eyebrows at me.

"Will it hurt?" I glanced from Ralph to Addie and then back again.

"It's nothing to worry about." She laughed, a soft tinkling sound that filled up the nervous air between us. "It's just going to be a small white bird; the same one Ralph has. He thought it would be special if you two got the same design. Is that all right with you?"

"You have one too?" I looked again to Ralph.

Nodding, he pulled back his sleeve to show off a small white bird etched into the skin on the inside of his upper arm.

"It didn't hurt at all," he assured me.

Ralph and I would have matching tattoos. In an odd way, I felt like it would connect us somehow. Maybe it would help bridge the time we had lost.

"Yeah, it's all right with me," I murmured, still staring at Ralph's arm.

"You know, Ava, this isn't a normal tattoo," Addie said, bringing my attention back to her and the task at hand.

"Because it's white?"

"Because it's magic," she corrected with a shake of her long hair. "With this," she tapped my bare arm where the tattoo would go, "you'll be able to leave town without losing your memory. It protects you; it makes you one of us."

One of us. "That sounds . . . good," I finished lamely. The emotion that suddenly gathered in my throat didn't let me say all that I was feeling.

"Here we go." She shook her hands out and set to work on the mark that would make me part of the town.

Excitement coursed through me, replacing the nervousness. As much as I liked to piss Uncle Ted off, I had never imagined myself getting a tattoo. Grinning wide, I let my eyes slide closed as Addie worked.

It was over quickly and with way less crying than I thought would happen. Running my fingers over the slightly raised skin, I was surprised at the tears that gathered in my eyes.

"Did it hurt?" Addie wrinkled her nose and ran her thumb over her artwork.

"No." I swallowed hard and tried again. "No, it didn't hurt."

"You know, I didn't even know Ralph had a kid."

"I'm sure he never expected me to show up on his doorstep."

Addie smiled as she packed up her supplies. "It's cute how proud of you he is."

Proud? Addie was wrong about that. We were getting closer but not on that level. I couldn't even call him Dad yet. But maybe this small white bird was the next step we needed.

"Okay, kids, I'm out." Addie waved from the doorway with two fingers.

"I'll walk you out," Ralph hurried to offer.

"I'm fine." She waved him away. "I can find my own way out. See you around, Ava." She winked, then disappeared into the falling snow.

"She's nice," I declared, still fingering my new art. "I like her."

"Nice tat." He came closer to inspect it.

"Thanks."

"Now it's official."

"What is?" I looked up at him.

"You're staying here."

"I was staying here even before this." I chuckled. Still, there was something warm about hearing it from him. He brought Addie here. Did that mean he actually wanted me to stay now?

CHAPTER 13

"Who did you have to pay to get study hall?" Toby demanded, kissing the tip of my nose.

"Everyone is in study hall," I scoffed, choosing to ignore his insinuation.

"Some people have tutoring this hour," he needlessly pointed out.

"I don't need it." I pursed my lips and tilted my head playfully. In fact, I did need it, but study hall with him was so much more amusing.

"It's fine." He kissed my pursed lips. "I'll tutor you later."

"I'm sure we'll study into the wee hours of the morning."

"Who talks like that?" His top lip snarled upwards. "You've been around Ralph too much. You're going to need an intervention soon."

"Whatever."

"Seriously though, I'll make sure you get an A in history." One eyebrow arched high on his forehead. "At least a C."

"Let's talk about something more fun," I pouted.

Toby caught my bottom lip between his teeth, sending shivers down my spine.

"What do you want to talk about?" he asked, letting go of my flesh.

"You already know."

"Not the Cold Moon Ball?"

"Why won't you go with me?"

"I haven't been to that thing in years."

"That's because you didn't know me."

"How about"—he ran one finger along my jawline, stopping to add a little pressure against my lips—"if I promise to think about it."

I knew he was trying to distract me with that magic touch of his, but thinking about it was better than the flat no I had gotten so far. "Deal."

Even if he didn't go to that dance with me, I was happier here with Toby than I had ever been in my life. Not that I had much to compare it to. Back in Montrose, I had thought I loved Caleb, but now I knew the difference—I barely even liked Caleb.

"Christmas is like three weeks away." Toby scowled.

"I know." It was hard to believe I had been in Havenwood Falls that long already. I opened my notebook to the first page, pen poised and ready to jot down a few notes. "Are you going to finally tell me what you want?"

"I already have all I want." He gently kissed my forehead.

"Very sweet, but I was being serious."

"Me too."

Christmas had never been a joyful experience when I lived with Uncle Ted and Jane. They bought me gifts, because they had to, but it was always awkward with them. I knew they didn't want to.

Now was my chance to make this Christmas better. I had Ralph and Toby. They didn't like each other, but they both liked me.

"What are we going to do for Christmas?" I asked Toby, trying to keep the childish glow out of my eyes.

"Probably the usual." He shrugged. "A make-out session in the backseat of my car followed by an awkward drop-off in front of your house."

"Toby. I'm being serious."

"Ralph isn't going to open his arms to me and invite me over for Christmas dinner."

"He might." Ralph was being seriously decent about my insistence on dating Toby. "He waved at you last night."

"He was swatting the snow out of his face."

My nose scrunched up. "I told you that wasn't true."

"If you say so."

"If I only had one Christmas wish," I held a finger up between us, "it would be for all three of us to be together for Christmas." They were the two people I cared for the most in the world. Of course I wanted to be with them.

Toby's low chuckle quickly turned to a full-blown laugh. "That is never going to happen, Ava."

"It could if you tried."

The feud between my dad and Toby went back too far for either of them to remember. Besides, it was never a personal issue with one another—Ralph just didn't like how Toby treated humans. And Toby wasn't like that anymore.

"How about we talk about something better?" He threw my own words back at me.

"What should we talk about?" I growled.

"On second thought, why do we need to talk at all?"

"The teacher will be back any second," I hissed, wanting him to kiss me anyway.

"And?"

Toby pressed his lips lightly to mine, applying pressure just as my heart was starting to speed up. My lips parted with a contented sigh, allowing his tongue to touch mine briefly. Much to my disappointment, he stopped the kiss before it could get too deep.

"I have an idea—one that you'll like."

"What's your idea?" It had better be good if he stopped kissing me just to say it.

"Let's go Christmas shopping."

"Shopping?" That was his great idea?

"In Montrose."

The furrow on my forehead smoothed out. Shopping in Montrose—that changed things. "Really?"

"Why not? You can leave town now."

"Ralph said I can't, though."

"'Cause he worries too much," Toby scoffed. "What can happen? I'll be right with you."

That was true. I hadn't been back to Montrose since I left it; I would love to go visit with Toby. Even if we did do some shopping while we were there.

"I'm in." I grinned widely.

CHAPTER 14

I inhaled a long breath of frigid air and held it in until my lungs felt like they were going to burst. Standing on the porch, too nervous to go inside, I chewed mercilessly on the inside of my cheek. How was I going to get permission to go to Montrose with Toby?

Oh well, I decided, *I can't just stand outside forever.*

"Hey, Ralph," I greeted in what I hoped sounded like a naturally high voice.

"Hello," he replied, staring at me from the side of his eyes.

Shit. He didn't buy my false bravado at all.

"What are you doing?" I sniffed the kitchen experimentally.

"Cooking." He held up his hot pads proudly. "Are you hungry?"

"Why do you always think I want to eat?" I scoffed.

"So . . . is that a no?"

Without answering, I crossed to my room so I could have more time to make my breathing normal. Pinching the bridge of my nose, I debated just giving up on the shopping trip with Toby. Maybe I should just stay and eat whatever Ralph was cooking. His food was usually good. It was Saturday, after all—a day Ralph and I usually spent together.

"Ava?" Ralph's voice called from the kitchen. "What are you doing in there?"

"Nothing." I frowned as I marched back out to him. "I was grabbing something in my room."

"How were the chickens?"

"Fine." Still terrifying, despite his best efforts.

"Hmm." He turned back to his work space. "Are you eating?"

60

"I can't." I pressed my lips together hard enough to make them hurt. "I already have plans, actually."

"What plans?"

"Christmas shopping."

He didn't say anything.

"In Montrose."

Still silent.

"With Toby."

He spun around, his lips pulled back into a smile that was anything but amused. "Is that supposed to be some kind of joke?"

"Depends. Are either of us laughing?"

"You're not going anywhere with Toby."

"We already have plans. It's not like we'll be out late."

"No."

"You can't just say no."

"I just did."

"Why can't you give him a chance?"

"Why would I?" He scowled, the lines on his forehead furrowing deep.

"You don't even know him."

"I'm sure I don't know him the way you do." I would have blushed at his words if they weren't so accusing. "You know how I feel about . . . him."

"He's changed," I told him—again. It didn't seem like he was going to believe me this time either.

"Do you think I want my daughter to be hanging out with scum like that? A murderer?"

"Stop calling him that."

"Ava."

"Ralph." This conversation was getting on my nerves. We'd had it too many times in the past few months.

"Regardless of your . . . company," he sneered, "you need to stay in Havenwood Falls, where it's safe."

"Safe from what?" Or whom? I didn't really understand why Ralph had come to this town to begin with. Who was he hiding from?

"You don't need to know all that. That's my business."

Ralph was hiding out here, and although he wouldn't tell me why, it couldn't be for something good. "You're my father. It's my business too."

"Fine." He crossed his arms over his chest and glared at me, a small vein throbbing in his temple. "I came here to escape the radar of other angels— fallen ones."

"Why don't you like other angels?" My eyes narrowed as I waited.

"They don't like me," he barked.

"Why not?"

"Don't worry about it."

"Tell me."

His eyes darted wildly from side to side. "I'm not . . ."

"Ralph, why are the angels hunting you down? Enough that you had to hide here?"

Just when I thought he wasn't going to answer, he blurted, "It's because of you."

As if his words physically touched me, I stumbled backwards. "What are you talking about?"

"Because you were born. These angels asked me to destroy you at birth, but I didn't do it."

"Is that why you left me behind?" I was the reason his angel pals were after him. I was the reason he had to hide here.

"I left you with your human uncle so you would be safe."

"How is that safe? I could have come here with you."

"I only came to live here about five years ago. It was best to cut ties."

"I . . . I need some air," I gasped, moving toward the door.

"Don't go far," he warned, as I slipped out onto the front porch.

Ralph blamed me for the things that had happened to me? But that wasn't fair. I didn't ask to be born. One thing was for sure: I needed some retail therapy with Toby. Screw what Ralph said.

CHAPTER 15

The pavement under my feet was slippery from all the snow that had fallen that week and was still falling even as I walked through it. I didn't know where I was walking to, but I knew I didn't want to stay in that kitchen with Ralph anymore.

I sniffed back my tears before they could fall and freeze on my face.

Behind me, a car pulled up and slowed down.

"What are you doing out here alone?" Toby called from the window he had rolled down. "It's cold out here."

"I just . . . wanted to walk." I shrugged helplessly.

"What's wrong?" His eyes were instantly alert, his eyebrows lowering down on his forehead. "Have you been crying?"

"I'm not." My voice broke and gave me away.

"Get in the car, Ava."

There was no reason not to listen to him. We had plans to go shopping anyway. Being careful not to start wailing, I opened the car door and slid into the passenger side. "I take it you're driving?"

"You still want to go to Montrose?"

"Of course."

His sigh was audible. "All right."

Besides his tapping on the steering wheel, we made the entire drive to Montrose in silence. He didn't even turn the radio on.

I knew from Addie that I could go past the town's wards without losing my memory, thanks to my bird tattoo that she had given me. Today was the first test of her words.

The only way I was going to get through this ill-planned shopping trip was if I didn't think about Ralph at all. His words rang in my ears, so it was going to be hard to not think of them. But I was willing to try.

For Toby, if nothing else. He was only taking me shopping to appease me.

"Phew." The air that I blew out made a whistling sound as it passed through my teeth. "I almost forgot how much more traffic there is out here."

"Yeah," Toby chuckled. "We get kind of spoiled in Havenwood Falls with no traffic at all." He expertly maneuvered into a parking spot in front of a small store I had never seen before.

"I've never been here," I commented as I joined Toby on the sidewalk. "What is it?"

"Secondhand store." He shrugged. "I used to come here a lot . . . a while ago."

"How long ago?" There was something elusive about his answer that immediately piqued my curiosity.

"When the new owner first took over. I think he was just over eighteen, inherited it from his grandparents."

The bell over the door jingled when we entered the musty shop, catching the attention of the old man behind the counter. He had to be in his eighties, at least. Looked like the grandparents still worked here too.

"Hey, Archie," Toby greeted warmly. The old man nodded but didn't greet Toby by name.

"Wonder if the grandson is here," I whispered, "so you can say hi."

"You mean the new owner?" Toby grinned.

"Umm . . ."

"That's him."

"You said he was eighteen."

"When he took over."

My face drained as I understood what he meant. "You knew this guy when he was eighteen?"

"Yep." My mouth fell open.

"They have kitchen stuff over here," he pointed out. "You should be able to find something here for Ralph."

All in all, the trip to Montrose hadn't been all that I hoped it would be. Toby was on edge the entire time, hovering over me as if I were about to be attacked any minute. We didn't go anywhere besides the old secondhand shop. Although I managed to find an apron for Ralph that said *Kiss me, I'm an Angel*, I didn't feel successful. All I wanted to do was get home.

"You sure you don't want to stop for food? We could go to Napoli's and grab a pizza."

"I'm not hungry."

"Tell me what happened today."

"Ralph and I got in a fight."

"Because you wanted to hang out with me," he guessed correctly.

"Do you know anything about fallen angels?"

"A little," he snorted, "considering I am one."

"There are . . . bad ones . . ." Did I sound like a baby? Because it felt childish to ask like that.

"They would say that we're the bad ones." He took a deep breath that made his nostrils flare. "Ralph would say that there is good and bad in all of us."

"What would you say?"

"I would say that it depends on which side of the line you're on." He glanced at me. "There is one of them that's after your dad. He goes by the name of . . ."

Toby's words were cut off by a car horn honking behind us. A car that hadn't been there just seconds ago. Its appearance caused a deep pucker to form on Toby's brow.

"Who's that?"

"How would I know? Just somebody cruising these back roads." On either side of us were fields that turned into mountains. We weren't far from Havenwood Falls; a few miles and we'd be within the wards.

Everything next happened very quickly. The car slammed into the back of our car and then pulled up beside us. I just had time to register that the driver was wearing a black mask before he rammed into our side, knocking us off into a ditch.

CHAPTER 16

"*Ava.*"

Goose bumps rose up on my arms and the back of my neck.

"Did you hear that?" I raised my head to search around the outside of the car for its source.

"Hear what?" Toby asked, still scowling at the back of the car that had run us off the side of the road, then peeled away.

"Someone just called my name."

"No one called for you. It's your imagination."

"This has happened before," I continued stubbornly. "I definitely heard it."

"*Ava.*"

"Stay here." His grip tightened on my shoulder. "Don't move."

"You did hear it?" I whispered excitedly. It was nice to know that I wasn't going crazy.

"I don't think they're here to play." He pressed his finger against his lips. "At least, not any game we want to play."

What kind of talk was that? Was he trying to scare me on purpose?

"Let's just go," I suggested, pushing my panic down. "Can you take me home? Will the car still work?"

"Yeah," he said slowly, not moving. "I'm going to look at the damage. Stay here," he ordered again.

"I'm not staying here," I hissed, getting out with him to round the front of the car. Several long scratches ran along the shiny black paint, but Toby wasn't even looking at the car. "What is it?"

"Well, isn't this a pretty picture?" a familiar voice taunted from nearby.

My eyes raced until they found the lone figure staring at us. How was it possible? Why was he here?

"Caleb," Toby called out to him before I could find my voice.

"Indeed it is," Caleb purred. "It's nice to see you again, Ava."

Toby moved quickly, deliberately putting himself in front of me. "Don't say her name," he growled. "Don't even look at her."

"Relax." Caleb rolled his eyes. "Me and Ava go way back."

"What did I just say?" In his anger, sparks of light flew from Toby's fingertips. "Don't say her name."

It wasn't really a big deal. I silently rolled my eyes. Caleb was never my boyfriend. Sure, I was a bit obsessed with him—who wasn't? But those feelings were never reciprocated. Toby was overreacting. *Don't say my name?* What did he think would happen if Caleb called out my name? Would I turn into a frog—or was I mixing up my scary creatures?

"I thought I was going to find just one little birdie out here." Caleb grinned—a large toothy thing that sent chills up my back. "But look what I found instead."

"What do you want?"

"You know what I want. Don't ask useless questions." His eyes shot briefly to me and then back to Toby again.

"How do you guys know each other?" I asked from behind my human— or not human—shield. "Caleb, are you . . .?" I let my question trail away, not sure if I should reveal that Toby was an angel and I was half angel. It didn't matter. Neither one of them were paying attention to me.

"What did you do, attach yourself to her?" Toby asked him. "You found her with her human uncle and you . . . befriended her?"

"A favor for a friend." He smiled in his lopsided way, the kind of smile that made my heart do funny things.

"A friend?" Toby repeated his words back to him. "What friend?"

"You wouldn't know him."

"Try me."

"Where's Ralph?"

"No idea."

"He wouldn't leave his bastard unprotected."

"He didn't." It was impossible not to hear the unspoken threat that emitted from Toby.

Unprotected bastard? Was Caleb talking about me?

Toby clicked his tongue against the roof of his mouth. "Actually, I changed my mind. I don't know anyone named Ralph."

He crossed his arms over his tight chest and glared at Caleb.

It was hard not to be impressed. Hopefully the two didn't decide to fight. They were both too perfect for violence.

"You really know how to irritate me, don't you, bird?" Caleb hissed.

Was bird supposed to be some kind of insult? It didn't sound all that menacing. It was probably best not to say that out loud, though, just in case Caleb decided to show me just how big and bad he could be.

Too sudden to be natural, dark clouds gathered over our heads. A streak of lightning ripped the sky open, followed immediately by a clap of thunder that had me cowering behind Toby. Maybe he had heard my silent musings.

"You don't want to make me angry," Caleb roared, raising his hands just as more lightning flashed.

"Holy shit." I took a small step forward, closing the space between me and Toby. "Is he making the storm?"

Toby turned just enough so I could see the side of his face. "I won't let him hurt you," he vowed. "Don't worry."

It was too late for that. I was full-out scared.

"You need to leave," Toby told Caleb, in a tone that made the hairs on my arm stick up. "This isn't a fight that you're ready to have."

"Is that supposed to scare me?" He cocked one eyebrow high on his forehead. "A lot has changed since the two of us last met." So they really did know each other.

Huh, I thought stupidly. *What a small world.*

"You heard me, snake."

Caleb's laughter started low, but soon his shoulders were shaking with it. "Snake," he roared with twisted humor. "I haven't heard that one in a while. Do you know what snakes like to eat?" he asked, suddenly sober again.

How could I have missed that he was a complete lunatic? All that time spent drooling over him and here he was—stark raving mad.

"Baby birds." He let the *s* ring out in a low hiss.

"Leave while I'm still letting you walk."

"I'm not going anywhere without the half-breed."

"That's never going to happen," Toby responded lazily, as if he didn't just call me a half-breed.

That meant Caleb knew what I was, before I ever knew. Was that why he wanted to be friends in the first place, if you could consider us friends? What did that mean? The implications made my head spin.

"Why do you want me to go with you?" I squeaked out. "We were barely even friends."

"I can assure you," he snapped, "I'm not after a friendly visit."

"I mean, we talked sometimes." I shrugged, trying to make sense of what was happening. Things like this didn't belong in real life.

"I would never be friends with someone like you," he sneered.

It was strange; I had never heard any words that physically felt like a slap. Until now. "Someone like me? What am I like?"

"You are an abomination, a disgusting thing that shouldn't exist." His top lip curled up, revealing two rows of sharp teeth.

"What is wrong with you?" I sputtered. "This is like, next-level evil."

"Oh please." Even from the distance we were apart, I could see his eyes roll up. "Why would I care what you think?"

"We hung out," I reminded him. He was always nice to me. How could someone lie so easily?

"I only kept you close to me for one reason." He held up one thin finger. How was it possible that even that finger was attractive?

"What . . . what reason is that?" It didn't matter, when it came down to it. He wasn't my friend or even someone I should have been talking to—clearly.

"Ralph."

"He won't come here. He doesn't even know where I am."

"Ralph!" Caleb flung his head back and screamed at the sky like a crazy person. "I have your offspring."

That was sort of an exaggeration. Just because he was looking at me didn't mean he had me. He was still at least ten feet away. I could turn around and run if I wanted to. Who was he kidding?

"If you don't show your face, I'll kill her."

That's a bit much, I inwardly scoffed. What did he think, we were in some old Western movie?

"I won't let you hurt her," Toby warned him.

"Oh, please," Caleb sneered, "you can't stop me. You gave up your powers."

"Not all of them." Fire shot from his fingers—fire that was easily blocked with a lazy swish of Caleb's hand.

"Any other tricks?" he taunted my would-be protector.

A light flared to life, a flash of light that momentarily turned the whole world around us to white. In front of me, Toby let out a string of profanity.

"What is that?" I had to yell to make him hear me.

"Just stay back," he ordered instead of answering me. *Typical.*

"I heard you were looking for me," Ralph bellowed from the middle of the field. He was just suddenly there between us and Caleb—he appeared from nothing. From his back, two enormous white wings had sprouted. My mouth fell open and wouldn't close. He was so beautiful. No wonder my mother fell for him. She didn't stand a chance.

Caleb's eyes lit up hungrily. "So nice of you to join us."

"Are you serving a new master, snake?" Ralph demanded.

"Never," Caleb hissed back.

"What are you doing here, trying to threaten my daughter?" Something shifted in my chest at his words.

"I've come for you, of course. You're a pretty hot commodity right now, worth a lot—alive or dead."

"No," I cried out, terrified of Ralph getting hurt because of me. Desperate to reach him, I clawed at Toby's arm holding me back.

"Stay back," Toby grunted. "He's got this."

"But Caleb . . ."

"Is no match for your old man," Toby finished for me. "It's best for you to stay out of the way in case things get ugly." As far as I was concerned, things were already ugly.

"You're a disgrace to your kind," Caleb jeered. "You don't deserve to walk the earth."

"Get some new material," Toby threw in loudly.

"Don't egg him on," I hissed through clenched teeth. Toby spared me one eye roll before turning his attention back on the two men in front of us.

"I'm here to make sure you get what you deserve," Caleb continued, his attention solely on Ralph and his impressive wing span.

"You think you're big enough to get that done, do you?" Ralph's head tilted dramatically to one side. "You should run along and find your daddy. Tell him you weren't big enough for the job. I'm sure he won't blame you." He shrugged. "Probably."

"I was big enough to find your offspring, wasn't I?"

Ralph's lips tightened.

"No one else could find her, but I did." His eyes were definitely giving off the crazy vibe. "I knew she was the way to you. You couldn't stop yourself from finding her." He laughed loudly. "I knew."

"You will leave Ava alone," Ralph ordered quietly. His kind of crazy was way scarier.

"Actually, I'll be finishing her off after I'm done with you." Caleb smiled widely. "I know an old friend of yours that will be very happy to see you again. You might remember him. Daniel."

A low sort of hum radiated off the name and swept across the field.

"We both know that isn't going to happen."

"You think you'll be able to get through both of us?" Toby asked boldly. Ralph's eyes flickered briefly to the pair of us. Evidently, we'd be talking about my choice of company later—after the crazy . . . whatever he was . . . was taken care of. I flinched at the thought of that conversation.

"I know I can."

"Enough!" Flames shot from Ralph's fingers and hit Caleb right in his chest. They weren't like the small flames Toby had produced earlier. Ralph's fire was blue and burned so hot that it seemed to singe the air it touched.

Caleb stumbled backward several steps, clutching the place over his heart that was still burning.

I slapped my hand over my mouth to stop my screams. Ralph was going to kill him. I mean, Caleb deserved to get his ass kicked for sure—but to be killed?

"Toby," Ralph thundered, "take Ava home."

What? "No way. I'm not leaving here until you come too."

I needed to make sure neither one of them got hurt.

"This has nothing to do with you," Caleb butted in.

"I'm the bastard offspring," I gasped. "It has everything to do with me."

"Does the worm have any say in matters once the fish is caught?" Caleb taunted.

Was he calling me a worm? The insults were kind of hard to keep up with.

"Come on." Toby took my hand and pulled me back toward the car.

"No." I dug my heels into the ground. "I'm not leaving."

"Don't make me throw you over my shoulder and force you away."

"You wouldn't do that."

"To keep you safe"—his wide eyes bored into me—"I would do just about anything."

"Is Ralph going to kill him?"

"No." Toby pulled more forcefully against my futile resistance. "He'll . . . convince him he's wrong and then alter his memory."

Before I had enough time to abandon Ralph and leave with Toby, the sky opened up and a cloud of fire descended down to join us in the field.

"What is that?" I breathed.

"Daniel."

"Oh my . . ."

~

I peeked around the bulk of Toby's car, where I had been exiled when Daniel arrived for the fight. The four men were glaring at each other so hard that I could practically hear it from my hiding spot. Daniel and Ralph both had their wings showing.

Despite my fear, I couldn't help but be impressed.

I felt split in half. Part of me wanted to rush into the fight to help Ralph and Toby; the other part of me, the part that was still human, was too afraid to leave the safety of the car. What if one of them got hurt?

"You have pretty good seats here," Caleb purred, crouching down beside me.

My whole body stiffened at his voice. "What are you doing?"

"I've been waiting for you for a while now."

"How sweet," I murmured from my dry lips.

"I feel like the big boys are going to be a while. How about you and I go somewhere safe?"

"You go ahead by yourself," I choked out. "I'll let them know that you left."

"Nice try." His false smile disappeared. "You're coming with me, half-breed."

"No, I'm not." Hoping to catch him off guard, I jumped up and darted around the car.

He was just as fast. His arm circled tight around my waist and clutched me back to him.

"How about we borrow your boyfriend's car?" he panted. Without listening to my protests, he flung me into the passenger seat and crawled in over me to get to the driver's side. "I'm sure he won't miss it." He grinned without amusement.

"Where are we going?"

"It's a surprise," he laughed, roaring the car back to life.

The sky was almost dark by the time Caleb pulled up next to a large building in Montrose. There were no windows on the side that I could see, just a large slab of gray concrete.

"Honey, we're home," he taunted.

"Where are we?"

"Montrose."

"I know that much." I rolled my eyes. I was scared, for sure, but a part of me still held on to a hope that Caleb wouldn't really hurt me.

That misplaced hope faded when he pulled a needle from a small case that I hadn't even noticed before.

"I don't want you spewing filth in there." He jutted his chin toward the mystery building. "You don't mind taking a little nap, do you, bird?"

"I won't say anything in there," I cried, panic setting in.

"Truer words have never been spoken." With one last dark grin, he leaned across the car seat and jabbed the needle into my arm.

"What did you . . ." My words slurred away, darkness pulling me under.

CHAPTER 17

*M*y head was throbbing wickedly before my eyes fully opened.
"Oh," I groaned, forcing my eyelids the rest of the way open.

The thought of him brought me more fully awake. I didn't recognize the room I was in, and it was too dimly lit to make out much of anything that was in it with me.

I was handcuffed to a small wooden chair. The shadows across the room from me might have been people—maybe. If Caleb was over there watching me, he would have known already I was awake.

No. I was alone.

Yanking hard on the cuffs, I knew right away I wasn't going to able to break free. I had enough experience with them to know how screwed I was.

A door high above me creaked open, flooding my eyes with bright light. Caleb stood there, glaring down a staircase at me.

"Finally awake?" he sneered.

"Let me out of here," I yelled, even if I knew the demand was useless.

"Where would the fun be for me then?" he asked, coming down the steps. "We're just getting started. What are we going to do with you?"

"You could let me go," I suggested. "I won't tell your boyfriend."

His hand arced back and slammed heavily against my face. As much trouble as I got myself into, I had never been in a real fight. The pain was surprising.

"You're not going anywhere. You and I are going to stay here and see if Ralph comes for you."

I experimentally rotated my jaw.

"If he got away from Daniel, he's going to come after you."

With one last kick at my shin, he went back up the stairs and left me alone again.

~

The room was so dark, I couldn't tell if my eyes were open or closed. The air whooshed loudly in and out of my lungs. In my entire life, I had never been so utterly alone. Even with my extra sensitive hearing, there were no sounds to pick up.

I swallowed hard, willing myself to stay calm.

Ralph and Toby.

I grasped tightly to my life boats. They were my family now. The only thing that mattered to me. Before I went to live with Ralph in Havenwood Falls, I was a mess. No one wanted me, and I didn't belong anywhere. Now I had a place to belong. I had a family.

Tears slid down my face, more tears than I had cried in a very long time. If Daniel killed Ralph, I would never get the chance to call him Dad. He would never know how much I cared for him . . . how much I loved him.

I had finally found someone that I loved, who might even love me back, and now he was being taken away from me. And here I was, trapped in some basement room by Caleb.

Helpless.

Why was I always so helpless with the things that happened to me?

The first time I talked to Toby was in the back of the history classroom, the day I decided to cheat on that test. He was trying to take my virginity. My chuckle turned into a sob.

Two months in and my V card was still intact. I should have let Toby take it when I had the chance.

Then again, it was kind of hard to sneak time alone with Toby when we had Ralph glaring over our shoulders. Even if he kind of accepted my feelings for my newfound boyfriend, that didn't mean he liked it.

Oh, I really needed to see if those two were okay.

And I was really, really tired of being the victim of my life. How dare Caleb kidnap me, drug me, and lock me down here like some animal? The only reason he was able to do these things to me was because I was letting him. I allowed myself to be weak.

Not anymore.

I took a deep breath through my nose and let it out slowly through my mouth. Concentrating only on the cool metal of the handcuffs, I willed them with all I mentally had in me to break in half.

I never expected it to work, but suddenly my hands were free from their restraints.

"Holy shit," I whispered, jumping up from the chair.

I wasn't sure how I had done it, but I was free, and I wasn't going to waste that by being all shocked like an idiot. In the next few seconds, I darted up the steps to the door where Caleb had disappeared. It was locked, of course. It didn't take much more than a small nudge with my mind to unlock it.

The door led to a very short hall with only one door at the end of it. There were no people there. Caleb never expected me to break out of that basement. I hurried over to the only exit and tried the handle. It was unlocked.

Just like that, I was back outside.

It was dark out, the air cold enough to make my eyes burn. I had no time to worry about that. I had no idea where Caleb was or when he was coming back.

I took off running without any idea where I was going. This wasn't a part of town I was familiar with, but I knew there were many different alleys all around us.

I didn't stop running until I was several streets over. Panting hard enough to make my chest hurt, I leaned against the dirty wall of the alley and wiped away the last remnants of tears on my face.

I was away from Caleb—now what? I didn't know how to find Toby or Ralph. I could probably find my way back home, but they wouldn't have gone there without me.

I closed my eyes and focused on Toby. *"Where are you?"* I whispered into the nothingness.

Suddenly, there he was, inside my head. I saw him walking along a street I recognized here in Montrose. I saw him as clearly as if I were there with him.

"Toby," I said out loud. In my head, he stopped and looked all around him.

He heard me.

"Toby," I cried out, excited by this new connection. "Meet me at the shop we went to earlier. The one Archie works at."

His lips moved, then the connection was gone. I would just have to hope he had heard. I flung myself off the wall and began running again.

CHAPTER 18

*I*t took me longer than I expected to find the shop. I had to first find a street that I recognized and then backtrack to find the shop. Luckily for both of us, I had a good memory and an excellent sense of direction.

Toby was already there when I stumbled to a stop in front of the locked doors.

"Ava." I saw his lips move, but I couldn't hear the words over the sound of my own breath echoing inside my ears.

My arms snaked around his neck at the same time his reached for me. "You came," I sobbed. "You really did hear me."

"You disappeared," his muffled voiced accused angrily.

"It was Caleb. He brought me here."

Toby's lips were everywhere all at once. He kissed my forehead, my eyelids, my cheeks, my lips. It made it hard to talk, but I didn't exactly mind at the moment.

"I was so scared," he murmured. "Scared that you were . . ."

"I'm alive. He didn't even hurt me." I was just bait. For . . .

"He's lucky he didn't," Toby growled.

Ralph wasn't with Toby. Why did only one of them get away? Surely, they didn't kill him, right? "Where's my dad?"

"Daniel took him."

Took him; didn't kill him. My shoulders sagged with the weight of my relief. "Where did he take him?"

"I know where they took him, but . . ."

"But what?" I gripped his arm tightly, willing him to tell me what he knew.

"You don't have to do that," he chuckled, poking my forehead with one finger. "I was just going to say that it will be dangerous."

"I don't care about that."

"I figured you would say that."

"Toby."

"I don't suppose there's any way I could convince you to go back home and wait for us there?"

"That is not going to happen. We have to go save my dad."

"Yeah, I guess we do."

"Where is he?"

Toby's sigh echoed through the air between us. "Being the bad guy is easier than being the hero."

"No one said anything about heroes." I rolled my eyes at his dramatic choice of words. "We just need to get my dad."

"Let's go, then."

~

"Do you remember the plan?" Toby hissed, his eyebrows furrowed to their usual height.

"Yes." We had only been talking about it the entire way to . . . wherever this was. This part of town wasn't a place I came to on purpose, but I had been here before.

I recognized the yellow door on the side of the brick building across the street from where we were hiding. Caleb had brought me here once. The details were fuzzy, but I definitely remembered that door. Whatever went on in that building probably wasn't good.

Goose bumps rose up on my arms as the chill in the air dropped several degrees.

"You're sure we can't fight?" Powers that I never knew I had were waking up in me. Maybe Toby and I together would be enough.

"I'm sure," he cut off my budding hopes. "I told you, there are too many of them."

How did he know? Daniel took Ralph; Toby came to look for me. It's not like he had X-ray vision and could see through the walls. Maybe.

"You're going invisible," he firmly reminded me, "and then going to get him."

Toby could go invisible, but he could still be detected by the other angels. Since I was part human, they wouldn't be able to see me. I knew the plan, and it made sense on the way here. Thinking about walking up to that door now was starting to shake my resolve though, in a big way.

My lips shook as I nodded my agreement. If this was the way to save my dad, I was willing to do whatever it took. Even if that meant going into a den of snakes. "I'm ready to go in there. If I don't come back . . ."

"Stop talking like that," he snapped, running a hand roughly down his face. "You're going to be fine."

"I was just kidding." Sort of.

Not really kidding, but when he looked at me like that . . . and just before I was going into that room where Daniel was.

Toby suddenly moved his hands to cup my face. "I love you, Ava." He kissed the shock off of my lips. "I'll see you soon."

"Yep."

I didn't give myself time to overthink things. Just like Toby had taught me on the way here, I gathered heat along my spine and down my legs and let it shimmer inside my chest.

"Good," I heard Toby mutter. "Hurry up. In and out."

Even if he couldn't see me, he had to have heard me gulping in air like a dying fish. This was it—go time. I turned away from Toby and half ran, half stumbled to the yellow door. Thankfully, it was unlocked. It wasn't even shut all the way.

Ralph was easy to spot amongst the stacked boxes and layers of dust inside the room. Careful to be as quiet as possible, I moved across the room and stood next to him. The biggest problem wasn't the chains that held him to the wall or the blood seeping from his leg and side—it was the two men standing in the small space with him.

Caleb and Daniel.

At the moment, they were completely focused on a paper taped to the wall. They didn't even turn around when I pushed the partially opened door further so I could come inside.

"Dad," I reached out to him with my mind, not even sure if it would work.

His head moved ever so slightly in my direction. My heart leapt.

"I don't know how to get past these guys." Toby and I made the plan for me to get in here and get to Ralph, but we didn't talk about how I would get back out.

From outside, there was a loud crash that finally made the two men tear their attention away from the paper.

"What was that?" Daniel boomed.

"I'll go look," Caleb quickly offered.

As soon as the door opened all the way, a huge ball of fire made him stumble backwards. "What the hell?"

Both men ran outside to investigate.

This was our chance.

"Don't worry, Dad," I whispered out loud. "It's me. I've come to get you out of here."

"It's dangerous," he hissed. "Hurry up and get out of here before they come back."

"I'm trying."

"Leave me," he snarled.

"Not going to happen." Using the same power inside of me that had freed me from the handcuffs, I made quick work of the chains around my dad. "Can you stand up?"

"I can see you."

My eyes locked with his. Strange how much of myself I could suddenly see inside of him. "You're not going to get all mushy on me, are you?"

"I just meant that you're not invisible anymore."

"Toby said that if I lost my concentration, it would interfere."

"Toby?"

"Let's just get out of here." We could talk about Toby later.

Ralph limped, but was still able to walk back outside with me. Thank goodness, too, because I wouldn't have been able to carry him. We didn't stop to wonder why Caleb and Daniel weren't out there waiting for us. They must have gone after whatever made that flash.

Which had to have been Toby.

"Toby isn't out here," I stated the obvious.

Ralph tried to help me look, but had to give up when his body fell limp. I managed to catch him before he hit the ground, but it was pretty obvious that we needed to get somewhere safe.

There was only one place I could think of.

"Come on, Dad," I grunted under his weight. "Let's get you home."

"How?"

"We can go see if the shuttle is around to take us back to town."

"And Toby?"

His name sent a spasm of pain through my chest, but I couldn't do anything about him until I made sure Ralph was safe. Hopefully Toby had gotten away and would be back in Havenwood Falls waiting for us.

"Let's go home. We'll worry about him later."

Ralph didn't nod. It seemed like even that was too much.

CHAPTER 19

"You're up early," Ralph said quietly, coming to join me on the large front porch. The sun was just starting to peek out over the mountaintops.

"I haven't been to bed yet." My voice came out as a croak after sitting in silence all night.

"Any sign of him?"

"Nope."

I had waited up all night for Toby to show up, and he still wasn't there. I had even tried to find him inside my head like I did in Montrose, but that didn't work either.

"Do you think he got away from them?" Even though I didn't want to hear the answer, I asked anyway. "What if he's dead? I shouldn't have left him last night."

"You did what you had to do." Ralph sat down beside me. "Toby knows that. He's fine. He will come back to Havenwood Falls, but he can't do that if he's being followed. Have patience."

"He risked his life to save us."

"I know that."

His change in tone caught me by surprise. I looked over to him. "I love him, Dad. I really do."

"I know that too." He nodded slowly. "I'm sorry that I put you in danger."

"You didn't put me in danger. I'm the one that left the safety of this town."

"Those guys were only after you because of me." He turned to look out at

80

the trees. "I didn't even know Caleb was around you. I've been watching, making sure you were safe, and I missed it. I hate that he . . ."

"Don't do that," I hurried to cut him off. "It's not your fault that the bad guys are out there."

We fell into silence, both of us uneasy with the mushy stuff. The sun broke free of the trees completely before he spoke again.

"I like when you call me Dad," he blurted out, then hurried inside to bang around in the kitchen.

My lips tried to curve up into a smile, but thoughts of Toby out there somewhere sobered me up again. Where was he? Was he hurt? If he didn't come back soon, I was going after him, no matter how much Ralph tried to stop me.

~

My eyes popped open at the first sign of light outside my window. Today was the day—Christmas. This was the deadline I had given Ralph for Toby's return. He promised that if Toby wasn't back by Christmas, we would go looking for him.

It had been a long few weeks.

"Dad," I yelled as soon as my head cleared my door frame. "Are you up?" I sniffed the wide array of food that filled the table. "Don't forget what today is."

"It's Christmas," a voice answered. It wasn't Ralph's voice, though.

"Oh my god!" My hands flew up to cover my mouth. Toby was there— just standing there by the door as if he hadn't been missing. "What are you doing here?"

"Ralph invited me." He shrugged, his eyes dancing.

"He did? When?"

"Back in Montrose, in that field. He said if we made it out alive, I was invited to Christmas dinner."

Tears gathered in the corners of my eyes. "We were coming to get you."

"No need." He held his arms wide. "I know my way home."

Running across the kitchen, I flung myself into his still-open arms and buried my face into his chest. "Where the hell have you been?"

Somehow he understood me. "I took a detour, just to be sure there were no nasties following me."

"I've been worried," I sobbed.

"I know." He laughed gently and pulled my face upward to look at him. "I don't know why you're so obsessed with me," he said softly.

"It's because you're cute." I sniffed.

He moved ever so slowly until finally, at long last, his lips pressed against mine.

Behind us, Ralph cleared his throat loudly.

"Is this Christmas dinner still happening or what?" He banged a large bowl down hard enough to make me jump away from Toby.

"Nice apron," Toby chuckled.

"Nice to see you too," he grumbled dryly. "Glad you didn't die."

Swiping the tears from my face, I scurried around the table to give Ralph a one-armed hug. "It smells great, Dad."

"Mmm." He scowled down at me.

But I knew he was happy.

And so was I. It had taken a while to get here, but I finally had a place I could call home. I might have to eventually deal with Daniel and Caleb, but for now, it was Christmas dinner with my family.

We hope you enjoyed this story in the Havenwood Falls High series of novellas featuring a variety of supernatural creatures. The series is a collaborative effort by multiple authors.

Havenwood Falls books by Amy Richie:

Paper Bird
Sun & Moon Academy Book One: Fall Semester
Sun & Moon Academy Book Two: Spring Semester

You might also enjoy these other books in the Young Adult Havenwood Falls High series:

Awaken the Soul by Michele G. Miller
Reclamation by AnnaLisa Grant
Avenoir by Daniele Lanzarotta
Falling Deep by J.L. Weil

Stay up to date at www.HavenwoodFalls.com

ABOUT THE AUTHOR

Amy Richie has lived in a small town her entire life. She lives with her three kids and their bird, Perry. She began writing in high school but never took it seriously until a few years ago. She enjoys writing because it takes her out of her everyday life and gives life to the people in her head. "When I was little I wanted to be a mermaid, then when I was in high school I wanted to be a vampire; now as an adult I'm a writer, which is better because now I get to be both."

You can visit her on her website: authoramyrichie.com

ACKNOWLEDGMENTS

Being an author can be a lonely road, so the people who are in your corner are exceptionally important. Thank you to all my family, my friends who are like family, my work friends, my book friends, the authors who continue to amaze me, and all the fans who show their support. Even a simple "how's your book coming along?" helps in a big way.

HAVENWOOD FALLS HIGH

Predestined

USA Today Bestselling Author

VALIA LIND

~ A Havenwood Falls Young Adult Novella ~

Predestined (A Havenwood Falls High Novella) by Valia Lind

From *USA Today* bestselling author Valia Lind—She goes on a hunt for answers, only to discover what she never realized she wanted until now.

Niccola knows two things: her mother has disappeared and she needs to find her long-lost father.

By some providence, Niccola ends up in Colorado, with nothing but a backpack. When she arrives at the small town of Havenwood Falls in the Rocky Mountains, she quickly realizes that her family's history is much more complicated than she ever knew. She's no stranger to keeping secrets, but even she's not prepared for what she finds.

While Niccola tries to unravel her past, she meets a gorgeous deputy-in-training who could be her future. She's spent her whole life protecting her secret, because being a half witch, half shifter is not something that goes over well with her coven. Yet, Warren sees past the labels and straight into her heart. She doesn't believe in destiny, but maybe she needs to rethink that.

Together, they must do whatever it takes to find the truth and save her mother. Time is running out, and Niccola must find it in herself to trust the town and its people, or lose it all forever.

PREDESTINED

BY VALIA LIND

Find your father.

For the hundredth time, I stare at the piece of paper with my mother's handwriting and the three simple words that shatter every notion I've ever had. I thought my mother hated him. I've hated him my whole life. Now I have to find him?

My mother's magic is all over the paper, but I can't tell if it's meant to help me or just residual from whatever happened here. We were supposed to go to dinner together. I ran out to pick up mail from our PO box and came back to my whole life ruined.

Looking up, I glance around the disarray that is our living room. The apartment is small, but we've lived here long enough to collect all kinds of keepsakes. Which are now thrown all over the area.

The panic I felt when I first walked through the open door hasn't really subsided. But Mom has taught me how to control it—and my magic—enough that I can keep a clear mind.

Whatever happened here, she's in trouble, and I have no choice but to follow the clues she left. Which is why I don't call the police or the coven. Instead, I walk over to her room, picking up a few discarded items, then I settle myself in front of our coffee table. After I flip it over back on its feet.

Next I light a candle, then I place my phone facing up in front of me. It's the closest thing I have to a black mirror, and I need it to scry. I pull my necklace over my head, the small quartz crystal dangling on the bottom. It's all I've got.

Holding the crystal in my hand, I close my eyes and set an intention. When I open my eyes, I place a tip of my finger against the phone, and ask for my mother's location. My body buzzes with magic, heating the crystal I'm holding. Leaning in, I look closely, studying the fuzzy image appearing on the surface of the phone.

But it's gone before I can make out too much of it.

"Come on," I whisper under my breath, as I try to force myself to stay calm and focused. The crystal heats up again, a town's name coming into focus before it's gone again.

"Denver?" I mumble, incredibly confused and a bit frustrated. This isn't giving me much information. When I try the third time, I end up with nothing but some mountains in the distance.

"This is useless!" I snap, sending some of my unchecked magic at the candle and throwing it against the opposite wall. Thankfully, the flame goes out, or I would be in so much trouble.

But that brings me to the problem at hand. I can't be in trouble, because my mother is not here to declare I'm in trouble. My chest grows heavy, and I try to keep my breathing centered.

"Think, Nic. You got this," I say out loud, just to hear a voice. Reaching for my phone, I open a browser and type in Denver, followed by mountains.

"Denver, Colorado? What the heck is in Colorado?" As far as I know, my mother has never been to Colorado. Or anywhere near it. I spent my whole life between California and Nevada. But if there is one thing she has taught me, it's to trust my magic. So that's what I'm going to do.

I walk over to my room, pulling out my backpack and stuffing three changes of clothes into it. After grabbing a toothbrush and paste, I search for my favorite lotion but can't find it anywhere. My body moves on autopilot, reaching for what I need, but my mind is completely on my mother.

What did she get herself into?

She's been acting weird for weeks now, but she wouldn't exactly share what was going on. Maybe I should've pushed harder and tried to figure it out. But I'm only seventeen. It's not like she was going to trust me with a huge problem, no matter how close we are. She's still my mother, and she will do anything to protect me. Of that, I have no doubt.

But she's gone now. And it's my turn to do the protecting.

Determination fuels my every move as I do another sweep of the apartment. Satisfied that I have everything I'll need for the trip, I swing the backpack over my shoulder and walk out of my room.

One last long look at the mess of our apartment, and I'm out the door. It's no time to be sentimental, or to let the feelings creep in. If I break down, there's no going back. I have enough problems as it is. Like figuring out how I'm going to survive a plane ride, since I hate flying.

~

It doesn't take me long to land in Colorado, but it's way longer than I'm comfortable with. Surprisingly, I got a flight out in just a few hours. Even though I tried, I couldn't sleep on the plane. My body is in constant hyperawareness; every person I meet is a possible threat.

With my backpack slung over my shoulder, I step outside the airport doors, trying to think of my next move. My eyes are instantly drawn to a pair of vans parked at the curb. They're nothing special, standard-issue passenger vans, except for the gorgeous images wrapped all around the body of the vehicle. Before I realize what I'm doing, I've taken a few steps toward the vans.

I freeze in my tracks, confused by this sudden pull toward the vans and the town painted on the doors. It's not like I'm sentimental about outdoorsy places, or unknown towns in a state I've never been in, so the only explanation must be magic. My mom taught me to trust my instincts, and my instincts are telling me to get in the van.

"Looking for something?" The deep raspy voice reaches me before the man walks around the front of the van. Dressed in a flannel shirt, jeans, and a leather coat that is much warmer than my own, he looks like what I would imagine my grandfather would look like. If I had one.

"A ride?" I don't sound sure of myself, so I clear my throat and try again. "A ride please. To . . ." I wave my hand toward the van's décor, and the man smiles.

"It would be my pleasure."

For someone who doesn't trust people, I find myself completely okay getting in the van with this stranger. I'm not the only one. A few people get in after me. I can tell they're human right away, dressed to go skiing, so I move to the back, keeping my eyes on them and the driver.

My hand reaches into my pocket to make sure my mom's note is still in there. I find instant comfort the moment I touch it. It's like a part of her is with me. For just a second, I let myself feel. The worry, anger, and emotions all rush in at once, and I have to keep myself from audibly gasping. Tears well up in my eyes, but I'm done feeling sorry for my situation, so I push them back. Along with the feelings. The only thing that's left is determination.

Maybe I should be more scared. Maybe I should be a crying mess on the floor. But my mom raised me to take care of myself, and a part of me thinks she's been preparing me for this exact moment. I may only be seventeen, but I'm no weakling. I will do whatever it takes to find my mother. Even if that means finding the man who abandoned us before I was even born.

~

I blink my eyes a few times, completely lost in my thoughts, when I see a sign flash by as we drive. I'm so out of it, the six-hour drive just flew by.

Welcome to Havenwood Falls.

Can't say I've ever heard of the town, but then again, I don't know everything there is to know about Colorado. The people in front of me are chatting away, but all I can do is stare at the passing trees. I don't even know what I'm doing here. Once I get to town, I'll need to do another spell to try to get myself out of this mess.

A few miles down the road, the town opens up below us. It looks like something out of a movie. I think that even more once we pull up at the inn. Everyone piles out, so I have no choice but to follow. The crisp late autumn air and the altitude hit me at once, and I pull my jacket tighter around me. I'll probably need to invest in something warmer if I'm to stay any length of time.

"I hope you find what you are looking for," the old man says as I reach to give him cash for the ride. "This one is on me." He smiles warmly, and for some reason, I think he knows more than he's saying. But before I have a chance to ask, he's talking to someone else, and I'm on my own once again.

I study the building in front of me, Whisper Falls Inn. The name is a bit strange, considering. Shouldn't that say Havenwood Falls Inn? Shrugging, I study the three story Victorian-style manor. It's gorgeous. Like something out of a gothic novel. A Christmas garland, red bows, and lights adorn the exterior. From where I'm standing, I can see a large tree in the front window. If I had my camera with me, I'd probably walk around the property and take some pictures. But that's not why I'm here.

Instead of going inside, I turn my back to the door. Right in front of me is what I can only call the town square. It's like this town stepped right off the front of a postcard. I shake my head as I start walking. The decorations are everywhere. Even the lampposts are sporting garlands and bows. My eyes are drawn to the large gazebo off to the side, with its lights and Christmas decor. When I look closer, I notice a few sun symbols and decorations, which makes me think someone here celebrates Yule. Snow blankets the area around me, completing that magical small-town look.

School must be out for break, because even though it's early afternoon, there are kids and teenagers everywhere. Thankfully, that means I don't stand out. As I walk, I can't help but feel like I belong here. I'm not what my coven calls a reader witch, so I'm not as in tune with emotions, but I do have a few reader talents.

With my own magic, I can decipher humans from supes pretty easily, and

I can tell this town is full of both. But I don't know how many of them are friendlies. I have to tread carefully. Glancing up, I see that I'm on Main Street. This seems like a perfect place to start, so I decide to head away from the inn.

The town square is surrounded by businesses on every side, each decorated for the holidays. From what I can see, there's everything from a music store to a pawn shop to a coffee shop. My stomach growls the moment my eyes land on Coffee Haven, and I realize it's been a while since I've had anything to eat.

When I step inside the cafe, the smell of coffee is instantly welcoming. But there's also an undercurrent of something otherworldly here. My eyes scan the area, landing on a few strategically placed crystals, pine cones, and candles. I smile to myself. Someone here definitely loves Yule. I bet norms eat this atmosphere up. But I'd be lying if I said I didn't enjoy it myself. It's nice to know there is someone like me here. Even though I'm not about to broadcast it.

"Hi. What can I get you?" The woman behind the counter is a few years older than me, with silvery hair and the most beautiful bluish eyes I've ever seen. Her voice is soft, and she seems friendly enough. I can absolutely see her as the one who placed all the crystals around the place.

"Hi. Could I get a caramel coffee and one of those blueberry scones, please?" I glance down at her name tag: Willow. She gives me a smile before ringing up my order, and I hand over the cash. The exchange makes me a bit apprehensive, since I have a very limited supply of money at the moment. Getting that flight to Denver took more of my savings than I would've liked. With that worry, all the others rush in. The only reason I would be drawn to this town had to be because somehow it would help. But I have no idea where to start, and the panic starts to set in.

Willow's demeanor changes just enough that I know she must've seen something in my eyes. Even though her customer-friendly smile hasn't left her face, she's studying me carefully. With a quick thanks, I grab my order and move to one of the tables. But I can still feel her eyes on me. Clearly, I need to be even more careful about keeping my demeanor neutral. Maybe they just don't trust outsiders. If there's a magical community here, I can understand that all too well.

It takes me five minutes to eat my snack, and then I'm up and out. A part of me wants to march back in there and demand answers. But I doubt Willow knows about my father or what happened to my mom. She might have her own reasons to be suspicious. I shake my head again, trying to keep the panic at bay. I need to shut it all down. I can't afford emotions right now.

When I leave the cafe, I just walk, looking for some kind of a clue as to why I was led here. I probably should've seen if there was a room at the inn before I decided to explore, but it's too late now.

When I stop in front of the old red three-story building, all thoughts of cold and homelessness are forgotten. There's something curious about the building, and when I look over at the sign, I read it out loud.

"Havenwood Falls High."

Of course a small town would have one of these movie-esque high schools, and something inside of me twinges at the idea of attending one. But this isn't why I'm here, and once the fascination subsides, the frustration sets in.

After taking a deep breath, I pull out my necklace and Mom's note, closing my eyes in concentration. My magic sparks as I try to see past what's here. I don't even know why I'm doing this, except that it seems like a locator spell would be a good idea. But after a few tries, there's nothing.

"Now what?" I ask out loud, wishing my mother were here to help.

"Now I think you should answer some questions."

I spin around at the voice, coming face to face with a gorgeous dark-haired guy. He seems to be a few years older, and definitely a few inches taller, than me. His dark blue eyes are narrowed as he studies me in turn. He's wearing jeans and a dark-colored shirt with no jacket.

"Excuse me?" I finally seem to find my voice. "Did you need something?"

Maybe I'm being a little rude, but the way he's watching me is making me uncomfortable. I've never had to use my battle magic as of yet, but my mom has taught me, just in case. There's something about him that's putting me on edge.

"As I stated previously, you need to answer some questions."

Purchase *Predestined* where books are sold.